The villagers said I resembled Joanna...

I was drawn to the balcony outside my room with a strange urgency. My eyes scanned the sea below—searching for what? But I knew. I was looking for a sail...for Joanna's lover.

It was her feelings that drew me to the knee-high railing. My arms stretched out to the past, yearning, straining.... I overbalanced and caught myself just before I hurtled to the rocks below.

What was happening to me in this old house... haunted by Joanna's presence, her portrait, even her feelings? What power did she hold that was leading me to some terrible unknown danger?

The Seventh Gate

DOLORES HOLLIDAY

Harlequin Books

TORONTO • NEW YORK • LONDON
AMSTERDAM • PARIS • SYDNEY • HAMBURG
STOCKHOLM • ATHENS • TOKYO • MILAN

Harlequin Romantic Suspense edition published July 1983
ISBN 0-373-33001-4

Printed in Canada

CHAPTER ONE

THUNDER RUMBLED from the clouds hanging low and dark over the surging, green gray Pacific. Although the air was warm and moist, I shivered as I glanced anxiously toward the dying mutter and quickened my steps through the sand and treacherous black rocks. I was tired from my long bus trip and wanted nothing more than to reach Seven Gates, the house on the coast of northern California that mother had left me, a house I hadn't known existed. When I had learned about it, it had seemed the answer to everything, for I was desperate for a change of scene.

Within less than two months I had suffered the loss of my beautiful, delicate mother, and had precipitated my second broken engagement. I had been the one who had called off the wedding and I was glad to be out of it, but Jeffery had not taken it well. Now I was drawing close to the house where my mother had grown up, and I was anxious to be alone and sort out the emotional turmoil in my mind.

I hurried to catch up with Miss Erna Dwyer. She had insisted upon accompanying me, and she still held the key to Seven Gates. She spoke for the first time since we had started out from her tiny house at the edge of the village, also called Seven Gates because my ancestor, the sea captain, had been first to settle in the area.

"Slow down, girl. You're going to break an ankle if you're not careful. I'll wait for you," she said, her leathery face gathered into a frown.

"But it's going to rain and if I get wet, I stay wet. My bags aren't coming until the bus station closes. The man there said he'd bring them then."

"It don't rain here in July," she said. "Leastways not often, and not today for sure."

Her flat voice left no room for argument, and besides, I was too tired to care one way or another. Frankly, I was disappointed. The fresh sea breeze I had looked forward to was, in fact, more like a sullen current descending down the sheer cliff face. Still, I rallied and pointed out, "It isn't July yet. There are still two days of June left."

She shrugged. "Rained once in July. It stormed something terrible the night Joanna. . . died. Twenty-six years ago, and Seven Gates hasn't been lived in since." Then with an abrupt change of subject she said, "Wish you'd given me more time to get the place in shape. Got the windows and doors unboarded, but I haven't had time to get much cleaning done. Pretty thing like you shouldn't have to move in with all that dust and spiderwebs."

My eyebrows raised. I wouldn't have thought she cared. Her attitude had been so taciturn and stubborn when it came to giving up the keys, I had assumed she had disliked me on sight. Her appearance had put me off, I had to admit. She was as tall as I am, but shaped like a long plank. Her hair was wispy salt-and-pepper with half of it defying the horn hairpins poked in to hold it in a small knot at the back of her head. I was used to city people, coiffed and shaved and crisply pressed into sharp molds. With Erna's slightly bent back, her beak of a nose and her fusty black dress, she reminded me of vultures I had seen perched and waiting on fence posts that had flashed by the bus windows on my trip from Chicago.

For a moment it pulsed into my mind that I must tell mother about Miss Dwyer before I remembered that I would never again need to embellish my simple stories to bring some little excitement into my mother's life. Her weak heart had put an end to her life, and her passing had left a big hole in my own life, as well.

"But there's no use crying over spilled milk." It was my voice breathing her words.

I blinked back threatening tears. Miss Dwyer had picked up the pace again and was a few steps ahead. I walked in her footsteps, lost in my thoughts.

I knew I had developed a penchant for dramatizing for mother's benefit after my father had died, but my latest fiancé had carried imagination to a point at which his insurance business was all in dreams of a rich future, while his appointment book was poor indeed. I made a good living from my painting for a greeting-card company, and I had begun to suspect that my work would probably be our sole support. If it hadn't been for mother's illness, I very likely would have married Jeffery within a few weeks after our meeting. His dark good looks, his dramatic and passionate spirit had rendered me breathless and quite insane. When mother had asked me to wait six months before marrying him, the time seemed a century. But with her lovely face taut with pain, her hands pressed to her aching temples, I could do no more than agree. Jeffery, of course, had gone into a fine display of temper, accusing me of letting her hoodwink me. He had said she only feigned illness, that her migraines were her way of keeping me at home. That insinuation had made me see red, and I had verbally let him have it. We made up, naturally, but his boyishly charming habit of turning his pockets inside out with an apologetic shrug had begun to wear thin. When I had broken our ringless engagement a few weeks after the funeral, he had raged that if he couldn't have me, no one would.

I wasn't afraid of him, but I didn't want to run into him at some mutual friend's place. I also felt I needed a change from the apartment, which dredged up too many memories. I could do the stylized Christmas trees and birthday roses for the cards as well on the west coast as in sultry Chicago. I had sublet the apartment and bought a bus ticket so I could save money as well as see the country. And now that I was on the western beach, my mind was still back where all my unhappiness had occurred.

Erna Dwyer's staccato voice brought me back to the present. "Look, you can see the widow's walk." She pointed a long bony finger up toward a cleft in the sheer precipice.

I stopped and stared. Again I was disappointed. The part of the house I could see looked derelict, gray and weather-beaten. My eyes moved down from the hipped and gabled top floor to the widow's walk, a balcony with a treacherous-looking knee-high railing. It was a big house, an ugly house, and I began to understand why mother hadn't spoken of it. It didn't appear to be a home that would foster fond memories. My gaze returned to the widow's walk after I had focused on the French doors leading onto it from the second-floor room. Suddenly I wasn't looking at the widow's walk; I was standing on it, overwhelmed with sadness, staring out to sea, searching for the white triangle of a sail.

"Well, come on!"

I blinked. Erna was staring at me, a half dozen paces ahead on the beach path.

I forced a smile and started walking. "We were a seafaring family. Although mother never mentioned the house itself, she did tell me about the old captain. She intimated he was a bit of a charlatan."

I caught up and Erna grinned at me. "So he was, so he was. Joanna knew all the stories."

"You knew my aunt well, then?" I asked.

"Went to school together. I worked for the family, but we were friends for all of that." She sighed, then made one of her lightning changes of mood and subject. "Here we are!"

We stood in front of a rusty iron gate at the foot of a set of steps chiseled into stone. I looked up the face of the cliff. The house was set too far back to be seen from here.

"Watch yourself. The tide has worn down these lower steps pretty bad," said Erna as she fished a big key from the depths of a pocket in her dress.

I held out my hand. Now was the time to go on alone. While my estimation of this strange old woman had gone up during our trudge on the beach, I had come here for solitude. My hand still out for the key, I said, "Thank you for seeing me to my gateway, Miss Dwyer."

"Just call me Erna. Everybody does," she said, ignoring my outstretched palm and inserting the key in the iron latch. "Took a good deal of oil to get this to work. I thought you'd have a car, so I oiled the gate to the road, too."

This gate groaned open and she held it while I carefully mounted the smooth, down-slanting steps. When I was above the tide level and my footing was sure, I told her, "I've never owned a car. In the city we have public transportation. Besides, I've always loved to walk."

She grunted a little as she closed the gate. "Can't say I love to walk, just never had anything but my feet to carry me around. Well, I think you'll like it here well enough for a while, but before long you'll be going back to your city and selling the house. Shame. It was a good house before. . . ."

We had come to the top of the steps and to the second gate, one set in a picket fence that seemed to surround the house. My irritation with Erna had increased again. I wished she'd refrain from telling me what I was going to do. I had thought I might sell the house when my need for solitude was over, but I didn't like having my mind read, so to speak.

Again I held out my hand. "My keys?" I askea pointedly.

"It's unlocked. Just lift—"

"I see it!" I said sharply, then regretted it. There was no use taking out my exhaustion on this poor old woman. Then I did some quick mental arithmetic. If aunt Joanna was twenty-three, my own age, when she died, and if Erna had gone to school with her, then she couldn't be much past fifty. Mother had been just a couple of years older, and though she had seemed delicate, she hadn't looked nearly as old as Erna.

Now the older woman closed the second gate behind us and I looked up for my first full view of my inheritance.

The house was massive and square. Its once white paint had mostly peeled and the picket fence surrounding it leaned this way and that. In the gloom of the gathering clouds it was depressing, with sand for yard and untrimmed shrubbery, but it wasn't the disrepair or the far-off thunder or the isolation that disturbed me most. It was the eerie feeling that I had stood here before, when I knew I had not. It was a curiously frightening feeling, somewhat as if I didn't quite belong to myself.

I took a deep breath and concentrated on the Victorian carvings of the porticos that served both to support the widow's walk and to span the arches of lacy woodwork across the wide veranda. I forced myself to look at the grinning gargoyles carved over the door, staring sightlessly out to sea. It seemed they mocked me with their eroded smiles, saying, "We know you. We remember. . . ."

I drew a deep, shuddering breath. Erna watched me, her face clouded with a frown. "Déjà vu," I said.

"Déjà what?"

"Déjà vu. The feeling that you've been somewhere before when you never have; that you're doing something you've done before. It seems as if I've stood right here, and of course I couldn't have."

The pucker between her agate-colored eyes deepened. It was obvious that this strange phenomenon had never happened to her.

We walked toward the front door and I rationalized for my own benefit as well as for Erna's. "You know, mother probably described the house to me when I was a child, and now it's coming back. It must have impressed me then, but I've forgotten since."

She nodded, but I thought she did it more from politeness than from real interest, and as she was losing interest, this was a good time to excuse her from what she obviously saw as her duty.

"I'm sure you have things you'd rather be doing," I said, trying a different tack this time. "And I really don't mind exploring the house by myself. In fact...."

"No, I better show you how to light the lamp. In the city I don't suppose you had much call for kerosene lamps."

"A lamp! You mean the house isn't wired for electricity?"

"Of course it is! But when I tried to have it turned on, they said the lines had to be repaired. The ones from the road running to the house. It'll be a few days. They were real sorry, but with the house boarded up for so long.... To tell you the truth, I wouldn't want to do without my radio and television, but it can't be helped. There's a motel, but it's five miles down the road, and with you not having a car and all...."

My wish for solitude after the crowded bus and my disrupted life of the past few weeks was becoming unduly important to me. I realized I was being obstinate, but I told her, "No, I won't go to a motel. This is my house now, and I've been looking forward to having some time alone. I need a complete change, and for a city girl this should certainly be it. But do come in and show me how the lamp works. Is there anything else I need to know? I suppose there's no telephone?''

She shook her head.

''Water?''

''Oh, you've got water, and you're on the waiting list for a phone. I ran the rust out of the pipes and had the gas turned on, so you'll have hot water. I lit the water heater; figured you'd stay. Stubborn, like Joanna.'' She grinned with teeth that hadn't always been hers.

I had to laugh a little. ''Was Joanna so stubborn? Maybe that's why I was named for her. Perhaps I was stubborn the moment I entered the world.''

''Named for Joanna? But the lawyer called you Lea.''

''It's Joannalea. Joanna for my aunt, Lea for my mother, Leanna.''

''I'm surprised Leanna would—''

Impatiently I interrupted her. ''If you don't mind, I'd like to have the keys now and learn what I have to about the house. It's getting late and the weather hasn't been improving. I still have to go back into town and get some groceries.''

''Why didn't you get them and have Tom from the bus station deliver them when he brings your bags?''

''Because I didn't think about it! I've been traveling for three days and nights without a bath. I didn't think about that, either, when I decided to see the world. Sorry, I feel edgy. I didn't mean to snap at you.''

''It's all right.'' Her deep-set eyes flickered over me, then she fished in her pocket and dredged up a handful of keys. We mounted the worn wooden steps and she unlocked the front door, flung it open and stood back.

Warm darkness like a sudden breath emanated from the interior and a curious dread made me step back from the draft of dead, stale air. My breathing quickened and I had to fight the temptation to turn and run back to the village to take the first bus east. I couldn't, of course. I didn't have enough money; Jeffery had been an expensive adventure, and it would be a couple of weeks before my check from the card company would arrive. Besides, I knew there really wasn't anything to run from; I was just dead on my feet, exhausted.

Erna was still waiting for me to enter, so I stepped into the dim hall.

"It ain't as clean as I'd have liked. The inside of the house is better than you might think from the outside. A little spit and polish and it'll look right pretty again." She went ahead of me and I followed. "Now, I put the lamp right here on the table. Soon as we get those colored-glass fanlights cleaned, the hall won't be so dark. Got any matches?"

I shook my head, and she dug into the pocket again and came up with two books of matches. "We'll leave one here. Now, watch." She picked up a kerosene lamp with a dull brass base and a glass chimney.

"Aren't those things dangerous?" I asked nervously.

"Heard tell of them blowing up; never saw one do it. I trimmed the wick and turned it up. Now take off the chimney and just light the wick, like so." She settled the chimney back on the old-fashioned lamp.

"And to turn it off, you just blow it out. To turn it down, just turn down the wick."

I was skeptical of my success with the thing, but I didn't say so. "Thanks, Erna."

"You'll get used to it. Here, you try it. I should have got you some food, but with the time I had, you're lucky I remembered the light."

"I'm sure I'll get used to it, and I do thank you for bringing it over." I scraped the match into flame and jumped back when the flame caught. Erna calmly replaced the chimney.

She turned to me and watched as I looked around the hall richly furnished in the style of the previous century, but without the fringes and fussiness that had made Victoriana so abominable. I caught her eyes and saw that she was staring unabashedly.

"You look just like her," she announced.

"Who?"

"Joanna, of course. Oh, I remember how the men swarmed around her from the time...well, I can't remember when they didn't. That milky skin—you better be careful in the sun here—and that black hair so long and thick she claimed it gave her a headache when it hung down. But she wouldn't have it cut. I used to help her pin it up. So beautiful."

She was silent while her eyes seemed to focus inward toward her own youth, and she looked a little as she might have when she was twenty. Then she stirred herself. "Ah, well, those days are gone forever, but you remind me. Even your eyes are like hers."

"Yellow—cat's eyes."

She grinned. "Joanna called them amber."

"School kids call them cat's eyes," I said, laughing.

With the light and the appearance of the dusty but beautiful hall, my moment of dread concerning the house had been banished and I was eager to explore a little, then sink into blessed peace and solitude.

"I'll show you to your room, then I'll be going," Erna said, once more reading my mind.

Some of my irritation returned. I'd humor her a little longer, but I'd choose my own room later. I trailed after as she took to the stairs, hauling herself up the banister like a sailor climbing his rigging. The illusion of the sea was further enhanced when I stepped into an upstairs room with a polished brass telescope mounted in a bay window. A waist-high globe stood beside the glass that pointed out to sea. A barometer hung on the narrow strip of wall before the window began. There were no curtains, but there were blinds to let down when the ocean was blotted out by the night. A framed map of the world hung on the wall to the right of the window. Pinholes marked countless journeys over its painted blue waters.

I touched the map, following the pinholes with my finger.

"Your grandmother and great-grandmother did that."

I nodded and went back to looking at the room. It was sparsely furnished: a tester bed with a narrow bit of crocheted lace hanging from its high frame, a pine chest gleaming with polish, as were the wide boards of the floor. A desk and a straight chair sat spartanly in the corner. A Salem rocker had its back to the bed and nodded to the sea breeze as Erna opened the French doors to the widow's walk.

I went outside, standing well back from the low railing, and watched as the sun stuck a skinny finger of light through the cloud cover.

"See!" shouted Erna jubilantly. "I told you it wouldn't storm today!" As she lifted her eyes upward, standing there like a flat, thin, latter-day Cassandra, the wind freshened and cooled, opening an ever larger hole in the sky for the afternoon sun. It struck her gaunt face and turned it saffron, smudged with deep gray shadows.

I shuddered as the breeze bit through my damp, sweaty clothing. I went back inside. Erna followed.

"Do you like your room?" she asked.

"Yes, I do," I admitted, but that still didn't mean I meant to accept it as mine. "Whose room was it first?"

" 'Twas the old captain's wife's. She stayed here when he was away at sea. 'Twas her that started marking out the ships' routes."

As we left the telescope room I noticed a door nearly opposite and I reached for the knob.

"No!"

I thought she was going to slap my hand. "Now just a minute!" I started to protest.

"That's Joanna's room!" she cried, her face strangely closed, as if she were expecting a blow.

"So?"

"You can't go in there!"

"Well, of course I can!" This was the last straw.

How could she think she could dictate my every move in my own house?

She stared at me, now barring the door with her wide body. "You don't know about Joanna, do you?"

"Know about her? She was my mother's sister and she died before I was born. What should I know about her?" I stood staring at her, my hands on my hips, anger rising in a flush to my face. My expression must have shown my inclinations, for she suddenly moved aside and handed me a key.

I jammed it into the lock and flung open the door. It was a rather pretty room, full of blond furniture thirty years or so out of date, but quite ordinary. I stepped inside. A storm of pain exploded inside my head.

"Oh, my God!" I cried out in anguish and stumbled from the room.

Erna slammed the door behind me and threw the key on a little hall table. Her face still had that warding-off expression and her hands shook so that when she put down the lamp, the brass base clattered sharply on the marble tabletop. Then she was gone, fading into the glaring, flashing lights before my eyes.

I staggered back into the room that had been chosen for me and threw myself across the bed. The dreadful pain began to ease and my stiff body slowly relaxed.

I spoke aloud into the empty house in a feeble attempt at comfort. "I never knew what mother went through. I won't—I can't have migraines. Now I know why people refer to them as splitting headaches." I lay still, afraid to move. My legs shook with the aftermath of the agony and the emotional turmoil it had caused.

Finally, after perhaps half an hour, I gathered myself together, found my handbag on the main floor and retraced my steps down the cliff. The solitude I had so fiercely desired was mine, and now I rushed toward the village, eager to be among people, even strangers, dreading my return to my new home.

CHAPTER TWO

THE VILLAGE of Seven Gates sprawled close to the ocean, with starfish-shaped arms climbing up the pine-shaded hill. I passed Erna's little white house, a park of white sand and dark green cedars, then proceeded up a gravel road toward the minuscule business district along the main road. The houses became larger as I moved higher, yet none came near the proportions of the house I had just left.

One house, I noticed, was decorated with gingerbread in a whimsical manner, reminding me of Hansel and Gretel. It was painted gray and the trim was candy-colored. A young man leaning against the porch post grinned at me as I passed.

Oh, no, I said to myself. *I refuse to even acknowledge his presence. Just what I don't need is another Jeffery.* But I couldn't resist a quick glance. At least he wasn't darkly handsome; this one was bronze, but probably just as dangerous. He leaned just beneath a swinging sign that read: P. McCarney, M.D. He certainly didn't look sick. How I envied anyone who could tan like that. He was too young to be the doctor, I decided. I turned away from his smile and quickened my steps toward the little market that also served as post office and community meeting place. Women holding grocery bags stood gossiping outside the dark shingled building; the men were inside.

The store was quaint and charming. Barrels held cheeses and pickles, while around the now cold pot-bellied stove old chairs were drawn up and occupied. I tried to avoid the eyes of the old men as they stared openly.

I gave my small order to the bespectacled, balding man behind the counter and he assembled my supplies, using a long pole with a hook to topple cans of soup from a high shelf. He deftly caught them as they tumbled down. Shortly I was on my way out with two bags heavy with milk cartons and cans.

One of the men set his chair down from its tilted position.

"So you're kin to Miss Joanna?"

I felt obliged to stop and admit the relationship.

I settled my sacks to a slightly more comfortable place in the crook of my arms and reached out with my foot to kick open the wooden screen door. The tall, gnarled old man stood up and took the bags from me. "You open the door. I'll carry your groceries."

"I can manage. Really, I can." I didn't care to foster a relationship with this rather disreputable-looking old man. He seemed clean enough, but rough and weathered in work clothes a size too big for him. But like Erna, he had a great capacity for ignoring my protests. He stood expectantly in front of the door until I opened it, then once again I was following.

"You walking?" he asked.

I nodded. "I'm taking the road back." I didn't think I needed to say back to where. No doubt the local grapevine already knew more about me than I did myself.

Crablike hands clutched my parcels and the man looked down at me from a stooped height that topped my five feet ten inches by some distance. He must have been close to six and a half feet tall when he was young. He walked with a slightly sideways gait, as if the wind always blew from the west, yet his footsteps in the soft sand were straight. He shook his great shaggy gray head.

"Too far and too narrow. That road ain't safe for walking." He shuffled off toward the beach while my indignant protest was still forming.

"But...." I gave up and hurried after him. "At least let me carry one of the bags."

"I've got 'em."

I could see that. I could also see that I was going to have him all the way home across that wearying sand and rock, so I set my teeth against further objections and trudged along beside him.

He introduced himself. "Elijah Caine. Knew you right away. Spittin' image of Joanna Brandt. If Elmer hadn't told me about you, I'd sure have thought I was seeing a ghost. Elmer, he's the lawyer. Lives in that big house there." He used his large, reddened nose as a pointer. "You met Elmer yet?"

"No, I've only met Erna Dwyer. She had the keys because she was getting the house ready."

He snorted and scuffed through the sand to the water's edge. "Easier walking here where it's damp. Packed like a regular sidewalk. Just have to keep weather eye out for the seventh wave if'n you don't want to get wet."

He was right. I directed a last bitter thought at Erna for making me slog through the soft sand at the base of the rising cliff, when I found my spirits lifting as Elijah strode along pointing out long-legged birds playing tag with the sea.

"Sandpipers. And those big birds flying low over there to the south, those are pelicans. Friendly birds once they get to know you."

The sky had cleared except for a few drifting rags of cloud in the west, and the breeze now blew fresh and cool. I took a deep breath of it and threw back my shoulders. I had been right; the change and time to think, to sort out my shattered life, would do me good. Maybe I would find that I could paint—really paint, instead of having to turn out those wretched greeting cards. The cool green of the sparkling ocean, the dark trees and the white sand should be inspiring, and the weather-beaten faces of the locals were marvelous portrait subjects. Perhaps here I could finally find my real self, instead of being what I had had to be in the city. There was no one depending upon me now.

"Yes, this is exactly what I need." I flung the words out to the ocean.

Elijah ducked his head in agreement and muttered, "You had to come back."

I didn't bother telling him I'd never been here before, it wasn't important. Anyway, I was beginning to feel very much at home.

I opened the cliff gate and waited nervously until Elijah had cleared the worn steps before I followed him. He lifted the latch on the second gate with his knee and went through. I found the key to the front door after a couple of false tries, then proceeded in after Elijah, who seemed to know where he was going. He went straight down the hall, then stopped so abruptly in a doorway I nearly ran into his broad back. I could tell by the stiffening of his shoulders that something was wrong.

"What is it? What's the matter?"

Elijah stood still a moment, then moved forward.

I stepped into the linoleum-floored kitchen. There was a round, golden-oak table in the middle of it—and in the middle of the table was a hatchet buried halfway up the blade.

Elijah put the sacks of food on the table beside the awful weapon.

"Didn't you lock up?" He didn't add that he thought I was a foolish woman, but it was there in his voice.

I nodded. I couldn't speak. I put my hands to my temples and a small moan escaped me.

"Headache," he said as he pulled the hatchet out of the table. The squeal from the resisting wood sounded all too human to me. "Got any aspirin?" he queried.

I nodded once more.

"Where?"

"In my purse." My voice was faint, but the act of using it put some strength back into my limbs and I fumbled for the pillbox. My teeth rattled against the glass he handed me. I recalled the terror my mother's migraines had brought her, and I fought to control my own.

"I just won't. . . it was just the awful. . . ."

"You'll be all right. It was just the shock." His big rough hand steadied me.

I forced myself to look at the gouge in the beautiful pedestaled table. "What a terrible thing to do. How could anyone—"

Elijah's brusque words cut off mine. "Could have

been worse. No use wasting tears on a chunk of wood. I can fix that so's you'll never know there was anything wrong with it. But look here, young lady—what do you think keys were made for? To use, that's what. This house has been boarded up ever since—for years. Do you think kids could resist getting into the haunted—"

"Haunted!"

He gave me a sour look but couldn't maintain it and broke into a grin. "Didn't you have a haunted house in your town?"

"Well, yes, I guess so. All overgrown and mysterious. Poor lady who lived there put up with a lot from us kids."

"Well, there you are. No use making more of it than a prank. Don't bother your head about it. Fix it as good as new tomorrow."

Privately, I considered any act that involved a hatchet and destruction of property to be more than just a kids' prank. Tomorrow I would see what Seven Gates had for a police force and make a proper report, but Elijah was probably right about its being the work of children. There was a Tom Sawyerish touch to it.

Shortly after Elijah left, my suitcases and easel were delivered and I was kept busy filling the drawers of the pine chest in the room Erna had chosen for me. I had peeked into some of the other bedrooms, and though I stayed away from Joanna's, I grudgingly admitted that she had, after all, chosen well. The other rooms were crammed with overcarved, overpatterned Victoriana and the bedsteads were so high that even I felt dwarfed by them. It was my intention to make a simple dinner, then go to bed early.

As I worked in the big square kitchen, the gouge in the table distracted me. Finally I looked through the drawers in a heavy oak sideboard and found a butter-yellow cloth to cover the damage. Then, with the lamp glowing in the center of the table, I relaxed as I ate my canned soup and cheese sandwich. Ruffled white curtains billowed in the breeze from the sighing ocean. It was a gentle, hypnotic sound, and I caught myself nodding. It was only nine o'clock, barely dark, but I went upstairs, the lamp casting cobweb shadows as I moved, creak by creak, up the steep, uncarpeted stairs. By the time I reached my room I was wide awake and jumping at the least noise.

Had I locked all the doors? Indeed, I wasn't sure I knew where all the doors were. I had locked the front door and checked the old sliding bolt on the back. Were there other entrances? I should have looked over the entire house before dark.

It was strange how one minute I felt almost as if I had come home after years away, then the next I felt like what I was: a city girl, strange and nervous in the country. I tried to fend off visions of the hatchet stuck in the tabletop and half succeeded.

I change from my wrinkled slacks and blouse into a tawny amber nightgown mother had given me because it matched my eyes, and spread the peignoir that went with it over the foot of the bed. I extinguished the lamp with a sigh of relief, still half-afraid of an explosion. The room filled with lazy, cool moonlight. The feather-down bed was soft and comforting, and I drifted off to sleep, lulled by the hush and sigh of the surf.

I awoke sharply. I was trembling violently, weakness washing over me in prickling waves. Was it a dream that had snatched me from sleep? I thought there had been a loud crash, but my mind was confused and in a turmoil. Shaking, I got out of bed, and after several futile tries I jammed my arms into the sleeves of the slippery nylon robe. The house was quiet and the moonlight was gone; it was totally black in the room. I fumbled for the lamp but couldn't find the matches. I had left them on the chest beside a candle. The candle would be easier to light.

A crash shattered the stillness.

"Who's there?" The words stuck in my throat.

Two matches, and I had the candle lit. I stood irresolutely, my damp palm slipping on the doorknob. I was afraid to step into the hall, afraid to stay in my room. I threw open the door and ran toward the stairs. The candle blew out and I stepped into a black void.

I SLOWLY BECAME AWARE of a deep cold. Teeth chattering, I tried to reach for blankets to pull up to my chin, but my plucking, nerveless fingers found only thin nylon. I opened my eyes and was swept by a wave of pain. The banister seemed to waver, then straightened. As I stared up the steps, my plunge into darkness began to come back to me.

"I must have fallen down the stairs." My voice was dry and raspy; my tongue felt too large for my mouth. I gathered the cold folds of nylon closer around me. At least my arms were uninjured. I tried my legs and was convinced that I was only bruised until I moved my right ankle. The pain brought a momentary nausea, and I lay there while the stairs seemed to swing back and forth like the pendulum of a clock. When at last they stayed still, I sat up gingerly.

"I have to phone."

"There is no phone."

It was a futile monologue, yet I gained strength from the sound, and I cautiously pulled myself up using the newel post, shivering violently.

"If I can just get to the kitchen and make some coffee. . . ."

I limped and hopped from banister to table to chair to stove. I clung to the old, long-legged gas range as the water began to heat, taking warmth from the flame under the percolator. The light peignoir billowed around me and I looked toward the source of the breeze. The limp white curtains blew far into the room.

"Oh, Lord! I locked all the doors and left the stupid window open!"

I saw what had caused the crash in the night. Two red clay flowerpots that had been on the windowsill now lay on the faded linoleum in shards amid clumps of dry gray dirt.

I moved to close the window and pain and blackness swallowed me up again.

CHAPTER THREE

"JOANNA!"

"Joanna?"

The faraway voices drifted in and out of my consciousness without meaning. I floated between two distances with faceless voices calling to me from both dim poles.

"I am coming. Wait for me."

"Joanna!"

"Come, Joanna! It's time you woke up!" A hand slapped at my cheek, and I reached to push it away.

"Ah! She's coming around. Joanna? It's Dr. McCarney. Come on now, wake up!"

My eyes were too heavy to open and I tried to tell them, but I wasn't sure if I spoke or merely thought the words. These people were so far away. And whom were they calling?

"Open your eyes, Joanna."

I lifted my heavy eyelids. "She's dead."

Elijah's craggy face swam into view. "No, you're not. You only feel that way." He grinned crookedly and glanced to the left. "This here's Doc McCarney."

My eyes haltingly followed his gaze. "Oh! It's you!"

The bronze young man smiled broadly. "Well, I'm glad to see you're back with us. Now, don't try to sit up. Can you tell me your name?" He slipped a pillow under my head and tucked a blanket closer under my chin.

"Lea Bond."

The sunny hazel eyes swept over me to rest on Elijah's puzzled face. "I thought you told me. . . ."

"I thought her name *was* Joanna. That's what Elmer said. Named after her aunt, that's what he told me, doc."

"Joannalea. Lea's what I've always been called." Again I tried to sit up, and again I was gently pressed back to the floor.

"Ah," the doctor said. "That clears that up. Do you know what day it is?"

"Tuesday? The twenty-ninth of June."

"I believe you're going to make it, Miss Bond. I can't find any broken bones. I think your ankle is sprained, but we'll have X rays to make sure. Want to try sitting up?" He ran strong hands over the ankle in question, and I let out a yelp.

"Tender?"

I glared at him and felt better for it. He was just too smug, too self-assured and much too good-looking to be a doctor. "I want to get off this wretched floor. I'm freezing to death, and my ankle's killing me!"

He laughed. "Nevertheless, I'm sure you're going to survive. You see, we couldn't move you until we surveyed the damage. But come, I'll help you to sit up."

When I was upright my head began to throb. "Oh, no!"

"The headache will pass in a few moments, I think. In any case, we're going to take pictures of your pretty head as well as your ankle."

"Must you patronize me?" He was right about the headache passing, but I found him an infuriating young man nonetheless.

"Was I patronizing you?" He sat back on his heels, his bright head cocked, a mocking grin on his face. "I see I must work on my bedside manner or, in this case, my floorside manner. Oh, sorry. Forgive my flippancy."

I raised my eyebrows but said nothing.

"Could she have a cup of coffee now, doc?" asked Elijah.

He nodded and Elijah handed me a steaming cup. I was still cold and the cup trembled in my hands. The old man crouched down and steadied my grip with his own.

"Now, Miss Bond..." began the young doctor.

"You can call me Lea."

He arched a bronze eyebrow. "By all means...if you call me Philip."

I nodded. The warmth creeping through my bones was mellowing my attitude.

"Can you tell us what happened?"

"Oh." I puckered my forehead in thought. "I was making coffee...no, before that...I woke up and there was a crash. My candle went out and I fell down the stairs. The flowerpots...."

"You should have lit the lamp; that wouldn't have blown out," Elijah noted helpfully.

"I don't suppose she's used to that sort of thing. I should think lighting a kerosene lamp in the dark takes some practice. Are you finished with the coffee? I'd like to get those X rays going."

Elijah took my cup. "I'll carry her out to the station wagon," he offered.

Philip shook his head. "I'll take her if you'll get the door."

I felt, and no doubt looked, a little dubious, for I was no mere slip of a girl and he, while tall, was very lean in his tight-fitting blue jeans. He grinned and pulled up the sleeve of his baggy gray sweat shirt and flexed an entirely satisfactory bicep.

I laughed and winced at the same time. "Okay, I'm ready. Have you got any aspirin?"

Elijah held back the screen door, and Philip picked me up in my cocoon of blankets and deposited me in the tan station wagon parked on the gravel outside the kitchen gate at the rear of the house. "I've got better than aspirin—after the X rays, which, incidentally, we do in my office. You've seen the place."

"How could I miss it? Those colors!"

"The latest thing for those Victorian monstrosities. Play up the fancy work."

"And the quaint shingle."

"Well, I try to fit the image of the country doctor," he said. "Sorry you disapprove, though."

"Well, you don't."

"Don't what?"

"Look like a country doctor—or any doctor."

"No? What do I look like, then?"

As the car crunched along the gravel drive to the main road, I thought a moment. "A college track star. On a scholarship."

He stopped and leaped out to open a rusted iron grillwork gate that matched the one at the base of the cliff, took the wheel again and turned onto the narrow blacktop road.

"That was number three—no, four. Elijah opened the picket gate for us by the kitchen door "

He gave me a quizzical look.

"Seven Gates. The house must have seven of them."

"Oh, yes, I suppose that follows."

Now that I was settled, my pain was concentrated in a dull throb in my ankle and I was able to look around with interest. "This *is* a narrow road. I see why Elijah recommended the beach walk."

Thick feathery pines reached long limbs across the winding road to entwine in a shadowy embrace above. To one side of the road the land sheered upward, thick with trees, and I caught a glimpse of a narrow, glinting waterfall. "It's beautiful country. It looks so peaceful," I said longingly.

"This is a nice drive, but one where you want to stay alert if you're driving." He leaned on the horn as the road narrowed around a steep hairpin turn; then the village appeared below, sprawling, white sanded and steepled among the pines, bordered on the west by the teasing, foamy surf.

"Lovely," I said as we descended swiftly upon the greeting-card scene. "I'll paint this, call it Pacific Christmas. The company won't like it; it won't have any snow. That's my job—doing cards. My ankle's swelling." I realized I was babbling, but I couldn't stop myself.

"It will, you know. Well, here we are." He got out and came around for me. It was all I could do to keep from nestling against his tanned neck, but I stiffened myself.

I would *not* allow myself to fall in love again, I thought furiously. Especially not practically at first sight. I had learned my lesson; I was just not lucky in love.

I freed my arm from the confining blanket and reached for the doorknob. "I'm getting very warm."

"Yes, but how would it look if. . . ."

I blushed. I had forgotten I was still dressed—or undressed—in my tawny sheer gown and peignoir.

Philip deposited me upon a freezing metal table. "And where do you come from, Lea?"

"Chicago."

"Ah, a city girl. Judy will be glad of that. I don't believe she's ever completely adjusted to country living. You two will be good company for each other."

There was a sudden stillness in my body, as if everything stopped for a moment. "Judy? Your wife?"

"My nurse."

A girl entered the room.

"Ah, Judy, there you are. We'll need pictures of her right foot and ankle and a skull series." He gave me a curt nod. "Judy will take your history."

While I alternately breathed and held my breath as instructed, I thought that Judy didn't fit my image of a nurse any more than Philip did a doctor. She was petite and beautiful and she wore her white uniform as if it were haute couture. When she had finished with the X rays she took my meager medical history in a bright soprano voice while I huddled miserably in my pilled, faded blanket. Then she disappeared, leaving me with my pain and a curious resentment for company.

After what seemed hours she bounced back into the sterile room. "Everything's fine. Here are the capsules for headaches or if the ankle hurts."

If, I thought.

"It's just a sprain—"

Just a sprain!

"—so I can take you home."

I didn't want to have her carting me home, but I had no choice. I said stiffly, "Thank you."

When the bandaging was done, Judy handed me a pair of metal crutches and ordered, "Follow me."

I hitched after her five-foot, swaying white form feeling like a lame Goliath following David. She drove silently and determinedly, pulled into my drive leading to the rest of the house and let me out. I was awkward with the crutches, losing my balance and nearly falling in the loose gravel.

"You'll soon get the hang of them. You can walk on that ankle as soon as you feel like it. You shouldn't need the crutches long. Eat lightly today."

Those were her parting words. I had none at all. So much for one city girl craving the company of another.

Seven Gates was not a silent monument to the past this sunny morning. Elijah's rusty voice bellowed an old sea ballad from an open window as I stood contemplating the back-porch steps. Four of them. After one nearly disastrous try, I got the feel of the crutches and hitched up to the kitchen.

The old man stopped in mid-song. "Welcome home, Joanna."

"Lea," I corrected, swaying dangerously.

He pulled out a chair for me to sit on and moved another up so that I could prop my foot. "Lea," he conceded, and indicated the shining tabletop.

I blinked, unbelieving. The gash was gone. He pointed out a faint patch that was a little more glossy than the rest of the golden-grained wood. "Don't touch it for twenty-four hours, then it'll be as good as new."

"That's beautiful! I can't thank you enough!"

He shook his head. "Nothing. Well, I want to get started on the fence. Thought by tomorrow I could have it all standing straight again. In a week you won't know this place—"

I broke in, "Elijah, I really can't afford—"

"Who was asking for pay?" His old face lit with a grin, then he laughed boisterously. "I want to do it. Say—for love. Why, maybe I'll shake the moths out of my old suit and you can treat me to one of those fancy meals at the hotel in Silver City."

I thought, *why, he's lonely. He probably hasn't any more family than I have. We two will have to stick together.* "I'd love to have dinner with you, Elijah, but you needn't think you have to. . . ."

His yellow white brows drew together. "Never you mind. Needs doing, and I got nothing but time." He moved to the stove and turned off the flame beneath the percolator. "Now, I think the coffee's ready."

I accepted a cup gratefully, as well as a breakfast of bread and jelly.

"I brought down some of your books. Didn't figure you wanted to try those stairs quite yet. Put 'em in the parlor. Now, you need anything, you just holler." He was halfway out the door when he turned. "And mind you keep your foot up." His big figure, a little clownish in the baggy pants, stumped off down the steps.

I dawdled over my coffee, thinking that while my dream of solitude had not yet materialized, perhaps I had found something better—a friend; perhaps more than one, though neither Erna nor Philip fell into quite that category. I wondered about Judy; would she be an acquaintance or a potential enemy? No, "enemy" was too strong a word. In an attempt at honesty, I had to admit that I saw her as a rival. Well, if, as I thought, she had designs on the young doctor, she needn't worry. As attractive as I found him, I couldn't afford the luxury of loving again—at least not for a long time.

I LAY BACK on an elegant Edwardian couch, a "fainting couch," I believe it was called by vaporish ladies of the last century. My book was unopened. The parlor had proven a jewel, richly decorated with the best of Victorian and turn-of-the-century furnishings that were beautifully set off by brown-and-gold velvet coverings. It was like being in another world altogether, so different from my chrome-and-glass city apartment. From where I reclined I could see the sparkling ocean, sun diamonds scattered generously toward the horizon, and I could hear occasional bursts of crusty song from Elijah, singing in tempo with his hammer. The only jarring note in my relaxed environment had no doubt been contributed by Erna; a modern white pitcher of deep purple, almost black dahlias. The oversized flowers so stiffly displayed might have been effective in Joanna's room, but they were all wrong here.

Joanna's room. A quick memory of pain, and I blotted out the episode upstairs and opened my book. I hoped the association would soon fade altogether, for I hated having a room in my house I was afraid to enter. I made a mental note to ask Philip about the migraines—if that's what they were.

The day passed slowly but pleasantly. Elijah came

in with a slightly dusty tray of hot soup, crackers and cheese at lunchtime. He was solicitous and fussed over me in a grandfatherly way that I loved, never having had a father's attention, at least not since I could remember.

Late afternoon brought restlessness and I decided a little crutch-aided exploration was in order. I was surveying the dining room, ghostly in its dustcover shrouds, when Elijah burst into the room, his crab-like hands firmly biting the collars of two dirty, squirming boys.

"Caught 'em peeking in the parlor window. No-good little tramps! Where did you get that hatchet, you dirty hooligans?"

"Hatchet? What hatchet?" the blonder, scruffier one queried with round-eyed innocence.

"Yeah, we didn't get no hatchet!" affirmed the other, forgetting to struggle as he stared at me.

Elijah growled, "Don't you lie to me! You two just run the beach like wild animals."

I thought he was being unnecessarily hard on the boys; after all, they were supposed to be innocent until proven guilty. I spoke up. "I think it'll be all right if you let them go, Elijah. I'm sure they can explain...."

He relaxed the grip of his hands, but not the grip of his strange eyes, which I noticed for the first time. One was hazy green, the other light brown. Held by that parti-colored gaze, neither boy moved; they just watched him nervously.

They were, indeed, two of the most bedraggled-looking ten- or eleven-year-old boys I had ever seen. The towheaded one was the taller of the two and the obvious leader, for the dark-haired lad just watched the other, waiting for his cues. I addressed myself to the leader.

"What's your name?"

"Mark Owens, and we wasn't doin' nothin'."

"Anything," I corrected automatically.

Elijah broke in, "Young scalawags!"

I looked at the boys, trying to see beneath the dust and scrapes and defensiveness. I decided, without much evidence, that they were simply adventurous, not vicious. "Thanks, Elijah, for apprehending my peeping toms, but I think I can handle it from here. I was just starting to explore my new home, boys, so if you two want to undrape the table and chairs for me, we'll see what's under there. Then we'll talk about your. . . prank."

"But Jo. . . Miss Bond. . . ."

"Call me Lea."

Elijah nodded but said nothing, just glowered.

I went on, "I really would like the company of the boys, and I think we're going to get along fine."

Indeed the leader, Mark, had already started dragging the long cloth from the table. "C'mon, Ollie! Grab ahold, will ya'?"

Elijah turned away from the industrious youngsters and grinned. "Well, you just remember. I'll be right outside if. . . ." He finished the sentence with a final dour glare in the direction of Mark and Ollie, then left with a wink at me.

Ollie, a Gypsy-dark urchin, uncovered a chair and I sat down gratefully as I felt around for another to prop up my throbbing foot.

"Suppose you fold that stuff later. Now, sit down and let's hear what you've been up to." I looked at Ollie, but his pink, peeling nose pointed to his friend, who had plunked himself into the armed chair at the head of the table and had clamped his grimy chin in grimier hands.

"Well, you see, it was like this. We were...we were...."

"The truth!" I said sternly.

He spread his hands and shrugged. "Aw, we just wanted to see the ghost up close. You know; if she was here. Not that we really figured she'd be walking in the daytime, but Ma caught me last...Ma won't let me out at night."

"Me neither," chimed in Ollie, his big dark eyes pleading with what I thought was a practiced appeal.

I was willing to bet that "Ma" had caught Mark Owens coming back inside after he had inadvertently pushed my flowerpots off the windowsill, but I let it go for now. "Tell me about this ghost."

Mark's eyes were of a peculiar sea green, and when he fixed himself to tell his story, it was impossible to look away. "I only saw her once; last summer it was. She was walking, kind of floating around on top of the porch thing."

"The widow's walk." I got a frown for my interruption of his highly dramatic rendition.

"Then she stood r-e-a-l still, staring and staring out at the ocean."

"That was when she started crying," Ollie breathed, obviously caught up in the tale, and collected a dark look from his leader's compelling eyes. Ollie subsided deeper into his chair.

Mark resumed his tale. "More like moanin' or wailin', I'd call it. It made my hair stand on end, I'll tell you."

His way with a story was making *my* hair stand on

end, and a prickle of fear and blatant curiosity waged a short war inside me. Curiosity won the battle. "How do you know this ghost was a woman?"

"Well, for one thing, it was a girl who got m-u-r-d-e-r-e-d."

I hated the sinister twist to his young lips as he drew every drop of blood out of the word "murder." Drama was obviously a big part of this lad's makeup.

"What did she, this ghost, look like?" I asked.

Mark's sea-changing eyes looked solemnly at me. "Just...like...you—"

I shuddered and started to protest, but Mark wasn't finished.

"—if you were dead and dressed in fog."

"Good grief! Where *do* you get your stories?"

He stood up with great dignity. "She did get murdered. Had her head split with an ax, she did! And my Ma says you're her. 'Carnated, that's what she said." He leaned forward and after a dramatic pause he half-whispered, "You're the spittin' image of her. 'Carnated!"

"Rein..." I said mechanically. "Reincarnated."

He stalked out, his straight, stiff back telling me that if I didn't believe him, he wouldn't sully my home with his presence. Ollie gave me a fearful yet apologetic glance and scurried out after his mentor.

I was left literally openmouthed. It wasn't that I believed in the ghost. It was obvious Mark's imagination was working overtime, no doubt primed by his "Ma's" leanings to spiritualism. But I had to believe in the murder. That would explain why mother had never talked of Seven Gates or said much about her sister, and it explained the half-finished sentences when Joanna was mentioned by the people who knew her. I realized that I had my hand clapped over my mouth, and clasped my two hands together on the mahogany tabletop. I remembered the other table. "Had her head split with an ax," that's what Mark had said. I prayed it wasn't the hatchet I had seen buried in the golden oak the previous day. It couldn't be. It was just too grisly even to think about.

I sincerely hoped I was not quite the spitting image everyone seemed to think. I was uncomfortable with that—a feeling that I didn't quite belong completely to myself. Again the vision of that awful hatchet intruded into my thoughts. From now on I would eat all my meals at the dining-room table, which bore no scar, however slight, of a split in its wood. I wished I didn't believe Mark's and Ollie's denial of any knowledge of that awful instrument, because if it wasn't a boyish prank, then what was it? I gave my head a violent shake. Perhaps I had just been royally taken in by a young but masterful storyteller. I fervently hoped so.

CHAPTER FOUR

THERE WAS a light tap on the kitchen door and the screen squeaked open. I jumped, and my foot slipped painfully off the chair.

"Hello! It's Philip. Where's my patient?"

"In here, the dining room," I called, rubbing at the pain.

He came in and took the same armchair Mark had so recently vacated, a fact I noted with interest.

"How are you feeling?"

I wanted to ask him how he tore himself away from the company of his beautiful nurse, but I bit my tongue, and as often happened I talked at cross-purposes with my thoughts. "Not bad. A little throb when my foot is down, but otherwise almost as good as new."

"And the head?"

"It's okay now." I considered bringing up the headaches I had experienced since my arrival at Seven Gates, but he was interested now, I decided, in the effects of my accident, not my general health.

He checked the elastic bandage. "Don't get it too tight. Just a little support to make it feel better. You're very lucky you didn't break something in that header you took. Well, I just thought I'd pop in since you didn't wait around till I could see you again this morning."

I opened my mouth to tell him how little choice I'd been given in that matter, then closed it on the words. Better to let him think it had been my idea to clear out of his offices. As it was, his sunny smile was warming me from my silly smiling face to my throbbing toes. Pride and self-preservation went out the window. "I'd ask you to stay for dinner, but all I have to offer is canned soup."

"Judy's in the car."

"Then you'd better not keep her waiting any longer," I snapped, standing with as much dignity as I could muster on my wretched crutches.

Apparently unperturbed, Philip said calmly, "I'll take a rain check—soon. Be careful on those things. They take getting used to."

"So I've been told," I said coldly, and retreated to my parlor.

I didn't have to do much analyzing of my feelings. I was just plain jealous, and I hardly knew the man. I was running true to form all right, even worse. At least in the past it had taken me several weeks to decide I was in love. I had just met Philip, but I couldn't deny I wanted an open field with him. And it wasn't even fair to him, for if ever there was anyone unlucky in love, it was surely I. No, I would put him out of my mind. After all, didn't most women fall a little in love with their doctors? It meant nothing at all.

I DOZED on my brown velvet couch under the open parlor window. I moved fitfully as tattered, half-awake dreams of Philip flitted through my mind, then I relaxed into a deeper sleep.

"Joanna? Joanna!"

It was dark, and I could see him only as a shadow against the night sea. He drifted closer and I heard him say, "I love you, Joanna." His deep, rich voice was thick with emotion.

"Don't go away." My own voice piped thin and was lost in banks of fog drifting from the oily waters.

"I...love...you...." He was drifting farther away with each slowing word, as if the ocean was drawing him from me.

"Wait! Please don't leave me! You mustn't go away!" My mouth screamed silent words that swirled into the mist and were lost. My body felt infused with love and longing like nothing I had felt before.

Suddenly I screamed and sat up looking around wildly.

Erna Dwyer stood over me, a wicker basket held in her bony yellowed hands. She moved one hand and covered her spare chest as if her heart was hammering as madly as my own.

"My, my! I don't know who scared who the most. I didn't mean to wake you up. I was being quiet as a mouse. Then you let out a shriek like somebody was killing you!"

My own hand was trying to quiet my frightened heart. "I'm not sure you did wake me. I was having such a dream! Anyway, I'm glad I'm awake, whatever did it." I trembled in the breeze that had seemed to suddenly turn cold as the brown-and-gold brocade draperies blew at the windows.

The lanky woman leaned over and closed the sash, then stood staring down at me. "Law, it near scares me to look at you. Just like Joanna come back."

"Please!" My shivering worsened; I felt as if something alien and cold had passed through my body and I pulled the old blanket up around my chin, then pressed my fingers to my temples as the throbbing began.

"Oh, oh," said Erna. "Looks like time for a pill. Doc said you might get headaches for a while. You stay right there and I'll go rustle up a glass of water. Your medicine in the kitchen?"

I nodded, unable to speak.

After I swallowed the capsule, I lay back and waited for relief. The sound of the surf in its futile runs against the cliff washed over me in gentling waves and my muscles relaxed as the tide ebbed. Erna had disappeared into the kitchen with her basket, and the subsequent rattle of dishes and silverware revived my spirits. I debated with myself the wisdom of asking her about Mark's fantastic story.

She poked her grizzled head around the door. "If you can hobble to the table...."

My stomach growled audibly, and Erna laughed. "Got here just in time, I guess."

I had to laugh, too, as I got my crutches stabilized under my arms. "Just barely, I think." Then my heart clamped on a cold weight. "Where did you set the table?"

"Why, in the dining room." She looked surprised that I should have asked.

I laughed out loud in relief and she raised her sparse eyebrows, shrugged and led the way to the table.

"Mmm, fried chicken. It smells delicious," I said, arranging myself and my crutches at the table.

" 'Tis."

"And that couldn't be a rhubarb pie!"

"Could. It was Joanna's favorite, and I thought... 'course maybe you don't like it all."

"I love it." I said it soberly, but Erna didn't appear to notice any lack of enthusiasm. I was tired of being constantly compared to Joanna, even though I was sure they all meant well.

The long windows were open and the curtains fluttered. I shivered in the cooling evening air.

"My, you're the coldest girl! Must be city girls have thin blood. Here, have some hot coffee; that'll warm your cockles. I'll light the candles, too. Nice warm light from a candle."

I accepted the coffee gratefully. "My cockles thank you," I said, deliberately throwing off the downswing of mood that had come over me when Erna reminded me of my look-alike aunt.

"Help yourself to the potato salad. That's also good for your cockles." She went off into her sharp laugh at the joke, and for a moment I thought she was going to slap her knee in her hilarity.

I tried and failed to join her laughter so switched to conversation instead. "Isn't Elijah joining us?"

She snorted. "Elijah? The day I waste my cooking on a man. . . ! I find myself lucky to be an old maid. Anyway, he went home. Did a good job on that fence, though. He's handy, Elijah is. Can fix most anything. A fisherman has to be handy. Never knew a boat that wasn't always falling to pieces somewhere."

I felt I had been accepted, if not for myself, then for my resemblance to Joanna, because the taciturn old woman had unbent conversationally. She hadn't referred to her abandoning me when I had entered Joanna's room, nor would I. We finished our meal while Erna talked about the village in the singular—*the* store, *the* service station, *the* lawyer, *the* doctor. Whimsically I added, "*The* one horse. . . ."

This time she did slap her knee as she snorted with laughter. "Just what Joanna said!"

I quickly changed the subject. "Elijah—I didn't know he was a fisherman."

"Oh, he ain't anymore. Retired. Actually, after he gave up fishing—oh, years ago, he went into business of some kind up in Silver City. Never would sell his boat, though. Still has it, but it's as old and decrepit as he is. Falling to pieces. Well, one day he was gone and then in a year or so he was back. Went broke, I guess. Now there I go, gossiping. Could be as he made a fortune and has it buried in that boneyard he calls his lawn. Wouldn't put it past the old codger. Doesn't part with much."

I smiled. It was funny her calling Elijah old when he didn't look any more weather-beaten than she did. I wondered with amusement if she did perhaps protest too much.

I played with my fork as I asked, "How old would you say Elijah is?"

She waved a deprecating hand. "Oh, seventy-five if he's a day!"

"Oh, surely not! He. . .seems very strong." I had nearly blurted out that he seemed no older than she.

"Keeps himself in shape working on the graveyard. Won't take a penny for it. Maybe he does have a fortune buried somewhere, the old pirate. Well, I better get cracking."

"Oh, don't go yet! I. . .I wanted to ask you about, well, a couple of boys told me I had a ghost. And that. . .that Joanna was murdered—with an ax." It sounded so silly telling it.

She turned a stone face toward me. "It's nigh onto dark."

"Of course. I shouldn't have kept you so long."

She was busy taking away the food, and I followed her along to the kitchen. "This will keep overnight. Can you manage the lamp?"

"Yes, thank you." If my dubiousness was evident in my voice, she ignored it.

"You better get to bed early. Rest will cure most anything."

"I will. Be careful of those rock steps down the cliff."

"Can't go that way. The tide is coming in. Have to take the long way on the road. Sure you'll be all right alone? If you've been listening to ghost stories. . . ."

"I'll be perfectly all right. Thanks again, and good night. Be careful. I'm sorry I kept you so long. I know that road is treacherous."

"Life's treacherous and I've survived it for fifty years."

Fifty? I did some calculating. No old-time romance with Elijah there. Perhaps Erna, too, had been as unlucky with love as I had been. I hobbled to the back door and watched her black figure disappear into the darkening twilight. At the edge of the shadowy pines bordering the property at the back it appeared for a moment as if she suddenly had become two shadows. I blinked and shook my head. An errant breeze must have stirred a small pine to make it look human for an instant.

I was drawn back to the circle of candlelight in the dining room.

"I think I'll just make do with the candles for tonight." I was startled at the sound of my own voice, loud in the hush. I had always had the habit of talking to myself, but here alone it sounded odd, out of place. I listened hard. The soughing of the ocean was part of the house sounds. What I missed were the domestic noises, the hum of a refrigerator, air conditioning, soft music from a radio, professional television voices touting panty hose or breakfast cereal. There was no traffic noise, no city-people noise, just the lonely climb of the surf and the crackings of an old house gathering night about its cooling shoulders.

I tested my ankle and was surprised when I felt only a mild twinge. I left the awkward crutches, picked up both candles and limped up the stairs. The flickering lights chased skulking shadows about the walls as I progressed, creaking step by creaking step, toward the top.

Suddenly I stopped, weak and sweating. In the gloom of the candlelight I stood staring at myself.

"No!"

My face smiled and flickered in the candlelight. I leaned forward toward the cloudy, dusty image of myself, then took the final few steps. It wasn't a ghost, it was a portrait of a woman with amber eyes, eyes wide with love. She looked through me toward someone, somewhere—her full lips curved in a wistful smile, black hair waved away from her face. My eyebrows winged up at her temples. It was a mirror of my face but not my expression, for this woman was passionate, vulnerable with love, clad in an amber gown cut low on her creamy white shoulders. She was strangely beautiful, strangely because although we might have been twins I didn't consider myself beautiful at all. It was her happiness, the fulfilled expression, that made the difference.

As I moved my candles her eyes seemed to flicker with life, and I felt cold fingers of fear moving up my spine. I glanced over my shoulder almost expecting to see the man, for I knew it was a man, at whom she smiled. I gave myself a mental scolding. How oddly I was behaving since my arrival at Seven Gates!

I leaned forward and in the feeble candlelight I made out the artist's signature—Jay Savage. An unfamiliar name, and it shouldn't have been, not with the talent displayed in this portrait.

I tore myself away from the canvas, my pain forgotten in my musing, and tried to rationalize my apprehension at finding my image at the head of the stairs. It had to have been there before, I argued with myself. But I was sure I would have seen it; how could I help it? Then someone had hung it today. Perhaps Elijah, thinking it would please me. Erna couldn't have done it—she hadn't had the opportunity. Or had she? And what did it matter? It was merely a painting, not an ax. If someone wanted to display it where I would be sure to see it, that was surely a thoughtful act. How could they know that just for a moment I would believe in ghosts? I was just tired and making much of nothing, I decided firmly as I entered my room.

I placed my candles on the beside table. Moonlight picked out the pattern of the white crocheted lace on the bed and slanted across the gleaming floor. I changed from the peignoir set I had worn all day to a white full-skirted nightgown. I deliberately avoided one of a honey color; I wanted to be as different from the portrait as possible.

It was warm and airless in the room, so I crossed to

the French doors and opened them to the cool salt breeze and the pound of the waves on the cliff. Yes, the steps would be awash. I wondered how many would remain dry. One could be cut off from the village by the beach path; only the long and treacherous road would remain open. It hardly mattered; if anything happened I doubted I could get to the village on my swollen ankle anyway.

I stepped out onto the widow's walk, wishing I had somehow brought both candles and crutches up the stairs, but if I stood with most of my weight on the left leg, the ache was bearable. Careful to stay far back from the treacherously low railing, I gazed out to sea.

A white half-moon hung over the black water, silvering a sparkling path as if millions of stars had fallen there. The sky was black velvet, deep and cool, studded with flashing diamonds. It was a lovely night. I saw all this, but I felt none of it. I looked at it, but it was like champagne gone flat.

I sighed and went inside, closing the doors on the night, and pulled the covers over my chilled shoulders. I blew out the candles and sought sleep. Tomorrow I would throw off the sense of oppression that had hung over me like a damp shroud ever since mother had died. Or had it begun even before that? Was it the flatness of my life that made me search too hard for love?

I wriggled deeper into the soft feather down of the bed. When I finally slept, Joanna wavered through my dreams, smiling—always smiling.

CHAPTER FIVE

THE MORNING, gray and aimless, matched my mood. Inside the chilly house I drifted from one thing to another much as the fog outdoors drifted in cloudy billows from the ocean to the straggly back garden to the pines along the road. I read, I stared out the dining-room window seeing nothing, until finally I settled into sketching.

It wasn't until after lunch—more crackers and cheese—that anyone came.

"Elijah! There's coffee in the kitchen. Help yourself."

"No. Thought I'd paint the fence today, but it's too damp. Have to wait for a sunny day. Just stopped in to see if you needed anything."

"I'm fine. It's a nuisance not to have refrigeration, but I'm managing."

"How's your foot?"

"Better. If I don't try to range too far, I can do without the crutches. Sure you won't have some coffee?"

"No, I can't stay. What is that you're doing? Why, it's the town. Now ain't that pretty!"

"I'll do it in watercolors, I think."

"Well, you're a real artist. I didn't know you could do that." His shaggy old head was cocked admiringly. "A real artist!"

"I wish I were. No, it's only greeting-card art, I'm afraid. Now, if I could paint like Jay Savage—"

He interrupted, "Savage? Pff!"

"And that reminds me—"

He went on as if I hadn't spoken. "You just need confidence in what you can do. You take my word for it, you've got more talent in your little finger.... Well, I'd best be going. Sure I can't get something for you?"

I shook my head and he was gone, leaving me alone with my little charcoal drawing in the middle of a charcoal day. "What I wouldn't give for a radio!"

I sighed deeply, gathered my drawing things together and went back to my book in the parlor where I stayed reading little, slipping often into tired thoughts, until I could, with a good conscience, make my meager dinner.

I had come here with some romantic idea of peaceful solitude, but what that solitude really boiled down to was loneliness—and boredom.

Darkness settled in early and it was with relief that I went upstairs to prepare for bed. I had left the candles in my room. I lit them and took one down the hall to an old-fashioned bathroom with the tub enclosed in a walnut base. I ran a shallow bath and managed to clamber in and out of it without incident, then got into the flowing white nightgown I had worn the night before. Back in my room, I pressed my nose to the glass and looked out. The fog was gone; I went out into the night.

A wind had sprung up and blew wildly, whipping my hair back, blowing my filmy gown into billowy folds. The ocean climbed the cliff and fell back, sending its salt wind stinging, awakening. I opened my arms to it and my oppressive mood fell away. I felt free, free of pent-up grief, free of all the Jefferys I had known. Just so had Joanna stood; passionate, fulfilled Joanna. She would have waited for her lover on this very widow's walk, her arms embracing the wind, that love-soft expression in her golden eyes. I let my mouth take the dreamy smile shape of the painting. Had she, too, looked out over the inky, star-strewn water, watching for a white sail or a shadowy figure at the cliff top?

How wonderful to be Joanna! My eyes closed with longing and it was as if another, more sensitive spirit settled into my being.

"Joanna...." The voice was light and cool as the wind. "Joanna...come to me...come away...."

The words whispered and whirled and blew away. I wanted desperately to hear and I drifted forward.

"Wait...."

"Joanna...Joanna...."

My knee touched the railing, and still I leaned to catch the whisper.

I was at the edge of the balcony. I was falling, my outstretched arms unbalancing me. I threw myself backward, panic tearing at my insides. I fell heavily, my shoulder blades striking the boards of the widow's walk painfully, but less painfully, I knew, than the concrete below. I lay there panting, the blood throbbing in my veins.

Dear God! What was I doing?

I got to my feet, trembling, my teeth rattling. I sank into bed; at first afraid to think. Then, as my shaking subsided, I forced my mind to function. What was it mother had told me?

"Lea, you must control your daydreams."

I had hurried that day to her bedside. All the way home from school I had been intent upon telling her about a recent incident. I was concentrating on the embellishments to make the story more interesting and I had walked into the side of a car. I wasn't hurt, for the driver had stopped for a light, but he marched me home and his language frightened me more than the accident.

Mother had warned me, "I suppose artists need more imagination than the rest of us, but you carry it to extremes sometimes, Lea. I know you often do it for me, trying to bring some life to me, trying to live for both of us, perhaps, but.... Oh, I'm not sure what I mean. Sometimes you get that glazed look and I wonder if you're not only painting a new picture in your mind but living in it, too."

I pulled the blankets up around my neck. I wouldn't cry. What good would it do? It wouldn't bring her back. I glanced toward the candles on the table—the wind had blown them out. The house was feeling the cold wind, its old bones creaking as it shivered in the moaning night wind. It would be easy to imagine it was Joanna coming up the stairs as I had, creaking step after creaking step, moaning over her lost love.

"Stop it! It's simply the wind and settling of the cold house."

I got up and closed the French doors and for good measure drew the blinds, then felt my way through the dark toward the bed. My groping hand sent something crashing to the floor. I think I screamed before I realized by the splintering of glass and the location that I had broken the barometer.

"Damn! I'll have to replace it." It was unthinkable not to. Seven Gates might legally belong to me, but I didn't feel I was its mistress, at least not yet.

The house quieted, as if by closing the windows I had warmed the bones and heart of it. I lay staring into the dark. I was nervous here alone—that was only natural. When I could light the old place with a simple flick of a switch instead of living flames that made me uncomfortable, fearful, I wouldn't be afraid anymore.

"Tomorrow I'll ask Erna to stay here until they hook up the electricity." With that reluctant decision made, I slept.

I LIMPED BAREFOOT on the cool damp sand, my ankle painful and swelling again. I stared at the row of tiny white houses all alike, all white, all neat and fenced with identical picket fences. Which one was Erna's? I had forgotten the number, thrown away the scrap of paper on which it had been jotted down. I was on a fool's errand in the first place. In the light of day my fears evaporated. Still, it had been a peculiar thing that had happened to me on the widow's walk; it would be better if someone stayed. I doubted that she'd come. Why should she? What was worse, I wasn't sure if I could make it back. I was about to give up and head for Philip's house to throw myself on his mercy when I saw the dahlias nodding their dark heads against the south wall of one of the set of houses.

Just a little farther.

I was standing on the second step summoning the nerve to take the last two when the door opened.

"Good glory! You look done in!"

"I am, I'm afraid. My ankle seemed fine this

morning and. . . I wonder if I could come and. . . ."

"You just sit right here in the rocker. Here, put your foot up on the porch rail. I guess wearing pants like a man has its advantages sometimes. Never cared for them myself. Then I never had your figure, either."

No, I agreed silently. I couldn't see Erna Dwyer wearing slacks. Her faded black dress was as much a part of her as her leathered skin.

The throb subsided with the elevation of my foot. "Elijah didn't come," I started.

"No, he mows the cemetery as regular as clockwork. Thursdays. I expect he'll show up at Seven Gates about noon if I know Elijah." She cocked her head and stared unabashedly. "Joanna attracted men just like you do, I'll bet." She spoke without emotion, flat words following each other and dissipating on the morning sunshine. Then, "What fool's errand brings you here?

"Funny I was thinking the same thing a minute ago. About the fool's errand, I mean." I stopped. She stared at me, hands on her wide, angular hips, her mouth folded in on her thoughts. I couldn't bring myself to ask her

"Had trouble with the lamp, did you?" she asked after a discomfiting silence.

I seized upon that. "Well, you might say that. I was wondering if you. . .until the electricity is on. . .if you'd . . . Well, I couldn't pay much. . ."

She broke into that grating laugh. "Proud, just like Joanna. Sure I'll come. I was going to, anyway. Have to finish the cleaning. Might as well stay and light your lamp and keep the ghosts at bay Bring a lamp for myself, too. Not that I'm afraid of ghosts!"

She contented herself this time with merely a hoot of laughter.

Suddenly I wanted to back out. I thought I could stand the creakings and moanings in the dark better than I could stand Erna's irritating presence. But what could I say now? I asked stiffly, "How much will you charge?"

She cocked her head, and with her black sleeves angling to her hips, she reminded me again of the desert vulture. "Heard you were an artist. You can pay me by painting my portrait."

Paint her! I almost laughed. I'd paint her all right! As a vulture with a near-black dahlia clamped in her beak!

The morning sun stabbed a shaft of light into her cavernous face, not quite reaching into the hollows, etching planes in sharp relief. Cassandra again! At once I was excited. I *would* paint her, I would capture that fleeting, eerie beauty in the ugliness. I would paint her as the prophetess of doom.

"Done," I said. "I will do your portrait!"

She nodded complacently. "That's settled. Now I'd better see about getting you home. Can't take you in my suitcase."

I winced as she laughed. She had assumed my ankle was giving me pain. "I'll get the doc. He can run you back in his car."

"Oh, no. . . ."

"Then?"

I shrugged and sighed. "When he's not too busy, perhaps."

"Busy!" She flapped her hand to indicate the sprawling little town. "Mighty poor place to start doctoring if you want to make any money." She produced a key from her pocket—it appeared she had a never ending supply—and locked the front door. "You sit right here. Be back soon's I find him."

I was thirsty, but that action of locking her door against me froze my request for a glass of water before it reached my tongue. As she flapped off in the direction of Philip's house the sun struck me full in the face. And it had been Erna who had warned me against sunburn on my fair skin. By the time she returned in the station wagon, not with the doctor but with his pert nurse, I was burning with more than merely sun.

"I guess the doctor was busy," I said, not bothering with a smile.

Judy answered brightly as always. "Not really. Hop in. No pun intended."

I clambered into the passenger seat to the incongruous duet of laughter from both women. I opened my mouth to tell Erna I didn't want her after all, but she shouted through her chuckles, "Be along soon's I can get there. Don't let any ghosts in meantime."

I huffed into place beside Judy and stared straight ahead. I felt about seven feet tall beside the petite blonde whose laughter tinkled like ice at a cocktail party. I listened silently as she lectured me about ligaments and tendons all the way home.

"Remember now—ice," she said in her bright squirrel tones as she tossed her golden hair.

"Of course," I said, my contralto voice seeming suddenly very bass in contrast to hers. Grudgingly I added, "Thanks."

"You're welcome, I'm sure." She backed the ungainly vehicle out of the drive with a sweep and was gone.

Where she thought I'd get any ice I didn't know or care. For all that no-good doctor knew, I might have really injured my ankle this time. It was puffed and blue-looking, and he didn't even care.

I limped into the kitchen, flopped at the table I had declared off limits and stared at the patched place. Erna had probably done it. Maybe she found some twisted humor in frightening me. Maybe she had even... no. How could I give a thought like that credence? She had liked Joanna; they had been friends. I reached out and touched the patched place. It was dry, and I wouldn't allow myself to conjure up the vision of the hatchet incident again. It was a prank, that was all.

But Erna. "A fool's errand," I muttered. "And now I'm stuck with it."

ELIJAH got there first.

"Hear Erna's going to stay with you. Don't envy you none. Tongue like a viper, that woman has."

There wasn't much I could say to that, so I changed the subject. "The fence looks beautiful, Elijah. How can I ever thank you enough?"

His craggy face lit up. "Well," he said in a deprecatory manner, "I'm painting it today. Got the paint outside."

"How much do I owe you for it?" Mentally I had my fingers crossed that it wasn't much. I really hadn't counted on spending money on the house and of course I would have to buy a new barometer now that I had broken the one in my room. I would have preferred that Elijah let me make the decisions about repairs, but what was done was done.

"Oh, I had it left over. Lucky it wasn't purple," he chuckled.

"Well, I'd still like to pay you."

He shook his head. "No need. Save your money."

"Well, thanks. I am in a tight spot with money right now, and I'm afraid I broke a barometer upstairs. I hope I can afford to replace it."

He didn't question the need to replace it. He nodded. "The only place to get one like that around here is Wilde's, unless you want to go clear to Silver City. I'd take you over—it's about five miles north on the main road—but I can't stand the man myself." He hitched up his baggy pants with his elbows and ducked out the door, a habit probably left over from his taller youth when it had still been necessary to duck.

Well, I thought, *Erna can't stand Elijah, and Elijah can't stand Erna or Wilde, wnoever he is.* For such a tiny community there certainly seemed to be a lot of hostility. Then I laughed aloud. I was one to prate about hostilities. I promised myself that the next time I met Judy Garnett I'd fall all over her with friendship. After all, she was a more appropriate person to be friends with than the redoubtable Erna Dwyer.

I proceeded to my Edwardian fainting couch, stuck a cushion under my foot and drowsed. . . .

The sound of a car woke me from my half sleep, and voices preceded the squeak and slam of the screen door.

Erna stuck her head in. "Don't bother getting up," she ordered. "I've got things to do." I heard her going upstairs and a door opened and closed.

Philip, resembling more closely than ever a college track man in a sweat shirt and shorts, ambled into the parlor.

"Hi."

"Hi, yourself. Is this a social call or are you doctoring? If you are doctoring, I don't need you." My heart did a high jump when he took my hand, and to hide it I scowled.

"My, aren't we prickly today! No, this is largely a social call, but I did bring you an ice pack." He backed away and held up both hands in a surrendering sort of gesture. "No charge, I promise you. The ankle looks pretty good, considering. I don't remember telling you you could run a marathon on it."

"I'll bet you were a miler."

"I'll bet you're wrong. Two and three miles were my thing. Don't change the subject."

"Your *nurse* said I could walk on it as soon as I felt like it," I said nastily.

"And you felt like it. Well, next time I'll give the orders. And be more specific." He pulled a small carved chair close and took my hand again.

I stared at the ceiling, and the quiet grew like a living barrier between us. Finally Philip said, "You don't like me. Why?"

I yanked my hand away. "Of course I like you. Why shouldn't I?"

"Why shouldn't you indeed? I consider myself quite a lovable fellow. And I like you very much."

I knew I was flushed, and the knowledge that I couldn't control it irritated me all the more. "This is a ridiculous conversation. Shall we go on and on insisting that we like each other or talk about something sensible?" I snapped.

He sat back grinning, the afternoon sun glinting on his crisp bronze hair. It looked warm and I wanted to reach out and touch it. I wished he'd go away, yet when he leaned forward as if he might get up, my heart closed.

"By all means, let's converse on a sensible level. You choose the subject matter. Books? The weather? Some other impersonal and altogether inconsequential matter?"

"Oh, Philip! Don't joke about it. You know it's because I do like you that I don't." My hands fluttered wildly, trying to gesture some sense into what I suspected was total nonsense.

To my surprise he didn't laugh. "Oh, I see," he said, as if he really did.

"That is, I have rotten luck with men. I pick stinkers."

"And you think I'm a stinker?" He was fighting a twitch at the corner of his mouth.

"Well, not yet, but. . . ." I denied the tears that backed up against my eyes. A great girl like me doesn't cry; it would be ludicrous.

He won the battle with the twitch. "I see," he said again. "You dislike me in advance because you've wound up disliking the other men in your life. Saves wear and tear on the emotions, is that it?"

"That's about right. It sounds ridiculous when you put it like that, but if you knew Jeffery. . . ."

"Jeffery?"

"My last fiancé. I've had two."

"Both stinkers."

"Don't patronize me, Philip. Your bedside manner is atrocious!" My temper was starting to rise through my moroseness.

For the second time he raised his hands in that attitude of surrender. "I'm not! I'm not! Those were your own words, remember? I'm trying to understand. You see, it's important for me to understand." He held both my hands tightly, looking straight into my eyes. "Give me a chance, Lea. I can't promise that someday you won't think me a stinker, too, but look at it this way. This time I picked *you*, and I've never picked a stinker yet. I'm afraid I'm falling in love with you—too soon." His sun-flecked eyes dropped, and he waited.

Silly hot tears swam into my eyes and I drew Philip's strong hand to my cheek. When his eyes met mine, I blinked against the threatening flood.

"You can cry, my darling," he said, his voice muffled with emotion.

"Cry!" I spoke brightly. "Why on earth should I cry? I'm terribly happy. You must know that. Anyway, I'm much too big to cry." As I chattered the tightness left my throat.

Erna clattered down the stairs. "There now, snug as a bug in a rug. Just like coming home. Same room I had when I worked here. It's down at the end of the hall on the right. How's beef stew sound for supper?"

A rush of gladness made me say with great enthusiasm, "Marvelous! You've no idea how quickly one tires of crackers and cheese and canned soup. Philip, will you stay? Is there enough, Erna?"

"Plenty," she said, bobbing her head up and down approvingly.

Philip had let go of my hand when Erna had started her noisy descent from upstairs. "No, sorry. I have to keep a semblance of office hours and I've stayed longer than I intended as it is."

My disappointment must have been apparent for he added, "But I'll come back after dinner, if I may."

Erna bared her whiter-than-nature-intended teeth in a grin. "We'll save the cherry pie till you get here."

"I'll walk you to the door," I said, hitching myself up from the couch.

"Never mind. You rest now, then tonight maybe you can show me around a bit. I like old houses, especially one like this where past lives have left their impressions. For instance, who would you imagine chose your couch? A woman who was perhaps somewhat indolent, who used her vapors to her advantage? Or perhaps a girl with a more-than-average romantic nature?"

"Or maybe someone who had sprained her ankle."

"Could be. I just like to know, or pretend I know. It increases my circle of friends no end and none of them ever disagrees. Very respectful are the dead."

"Well, tonight I'll increase your circle by at least one more. I'll introduce you to my Aunt Joanna."

"I'll be charmed, I'm sure. Now I'm off. See you around eight."

As Erna hadn't moved or even stopped grinning until I mentioned the upcoming introduction, we parted with no more than stiff little waves. When he was gone Erna spoke.

"What did you mean—introduce Joanna?"

"Her picture, of course."

A series of fleeting expressions chased each other over her leathery countenance, each one more inscrutable than the one before. "Oh," she said, then, shaking her head, she plodded in her black oxfords back toward the kitchen. Disapproval was manifested in the stiffness of her retreating back.

I frowned and shook my own head. If I lived to be a thousand I would never understand this queer person, and I heartily wished I had never asked her to come. Still, it was better to have someone in the house with me at night, though I was certain I would have no more strange episodes such as my near tragedy on the widow's walk.

I spent the remainder of the afternoon dreaming of Philip and visualizing ancestors to match various pieces of parlor furniture. The little rosewood chair so intricately carved would have been chosen by a lady—someone like my mother—small, blond and gentle. The big wooden armchair with its faded, whiskery upholstery on the seat—that would have belonged to a wheezing uncle type. There were his pipes beside it and a no-nonsense tobacco jar with a tarnished metal lid on a straight-up-and-down table. There had been no attempt to make the room conform to any particular period. Those who had lived here had simply added whatever had been popular in their generations. Philip was right. These friends were quite wonderful; they made the day pass quickly.

ERNA'S CHERRY PIE was delicious, and to give her credit, when she had eaten her own she went off and left Philip and me together.

"Is there a room more comfortable than your romantic front parlor, do you think? I was hoping for a nice comfortable sofa, you know." He held my hand across the shining expanse of mahogany.

"I don't know. I certainly hope so," I said before I thought.

Philip arched an eyebrow and leered at me, then

laughed and came to help me up. "Come on, I imagine there must be a second parlor on the other side. Shall we have a look?"

He encircled my waist with his arm and took some of my weight off my ankle as we progressed to a door at the foot of the stairs. His warmth and closeness and the musky male smell of him squeezed my heart until I could scarcely breathe. All I longed for was to have both of his arms around me and to lose myself in his kisses. As he predicted, there was another parlor, furnished in a more modern manner, but I was in no mood to take notice of the style.

"Aha, a sofa!"

I believe his lips claimed mine before we were settled. At least I have no memory of crossing the room and sitting. At last he gently pushed me back to arm's length and tipped up my chin with his finger. "You know, I don't believe in love at first sight."

"Neither do I," I said mendaciously, for while I never had, tonight had changed my belief decidedly.

"But when I saw you picking your way so carefully among the rocks—"

"And slogging along so tiredly through that damned loose sand...."

"—when it would have been so much easier to have walked on the hard-packed sand by the water...no, you've got me off the track. But I did think you needed someone to take care of you."

"What, a big girl like me!"

"You don't like being tall." It wasn't a question, it was a statement.

"Oh, it has its advantages. 'Lea, dear, would you reach me that little jam jar off the top shelf. You're so tall.' No, I guess I don't really mind. I understand

I get it from my aunt. Oh, that's right, I was going to introduce you two. Come along. She's at the top of the stairs. If you'll bring the lamp.... Philip! Erna put that lamp in here. How did she know...?"

"Even Erna was young once," Philip smiled as he lifted the lamp from a step table beside the sofa I now noted was a long curved affair.

"Do you think so? I rather doubt it," I whispered, in case she was hovering nearby. We were laughing as we started up the stairs, Philip ahead, me gripping the banister to aid my hobbling ascent.

"Isn't she something?" I asked as Philip gained the landing.

"I must have misunderstood you, Lea. I thought you said she was at the head of the stairs."

"Why, she is. Philip! She's gone! The painting...."

"Are you sure it was here?"

"Positive! Someone must have moved it again."

"Again?"

"Well, it wasn't there and then it was...and now it's gone. I'm not making any sense. It's just...why do they keep moving it?"

Philip was holding the lamp close to the faded gold-striped wallpaper, then he passed his sensitive fingers over the wall. He didn't turn back to me for a few moments and when he did he said, "Well, since I'm not to meet the lovely Joanna after all, suppose we find out if there's another piece of that pie around."

I followed him back down the stairs. "You don't believe me, do you, that she—the painting—was ever really there? That's what you were feeling for, wasn't it? The nail?"

"I think you might have been mistaken. After all, it's a strange house to you. You must have seen it hanging in another place, perhaps at the top of the third-story stairs."

"No," I insisted stubbornly. "It was there. I haven't had a chance to go to the top of the house yet. It was there, Philip. It was!"

He put his arm around me and gave me a reassuring squeeze. "Let's not make a big thing of it. It's not important."

"Yes, it is. It's important because you don't believe me."

"Lea," he said gently, "there is no nail, not even a hole where there might have been one."

My throat was closing on a familiar pain. "It was there!"

"All right, darling. All right. Now, please, let's find that cherry pie." He raised his voice. "Erna!"

"No need to shout. I'm right here in the kitchen. Figured you'd want some fresh coffee, too."

Dispiritedly I let Philip take me into the weak yellow light of the kitchen and to the aroma of steaming coffee. He and Erna talked and laughed a bit feverishly, I thought, and then he was gone, having made no effort at all to kiss me goodbye. A perfunctory wave and I was left alone with my weathered Cassandra. When Philip had gone she was silent, her deep eyes not looking outward but seeming to be focused on her thoughts.

"I'm going to bed," I said snappishly.

"Good idea."

She didn't move, so I picked up one of the lamps and pulled myself up the banister to the top of the stairs. I stood staring at the place where Joanna had been. Well, she was no longer there and I had found out something important about my new love. Exactly why he should have believed me over the evidence, I wasn't sure. I only knew that I was disappointed already.

Wearily I undressed and slipped into bed. It was while I was waiting for blessed eradicating sleep that I began to doubt. What if it had never been there at all? What if she. . . what if. . . ?

I remembered how Erna had locked her door against me, making me wait on the porch. It was a queer woman indeed that I had chosen for a companion. What was she hiding in that little clapboard house?

"Oh, stop this!" I whispered to myself. "You make too much of things."

CHAPTER SIX

I DIDN'T get up right away the next morning. I lay awhile pondering my strange feelings: the déjà vu, the disappearing portrait, Philip—too much feeling, too soon. Yet there was an emptiness, too. Mother, of course. She had taken up a lot of my life.

"You'd have made a fine nurse," she'd say, as I pressed a cold compress to her head.

"I'd have hated nursing!" I told the morning-cold room and threw back the blankets with a vengeance. I dressed quickly and went downstairs to be greeted by a note propped against a sugar bowl full of silver spoons.

> Went into village. Coffee still hot if you don't sleep till noon.
>
> E.

It was at least still warm and I took a cup into the dining room. I started to plan my day—work on the greeting-card designs....

Still, I sat doing nothing, unable to move, my thoughts returning always to Philip, and each time I wrenched them away.

"I should explore the house. Go treasure hunting. Better still, find Joanna and prove to Philip... what?" No matter where the painting was, the fact remained that it wasn't where it ought to be—at the head of the stairs where I had seen it. Or had I?

Finally I returned my coffee cup to the kitchen and trailed slowly up the stairs, staring at the place where I had seen Joanna flickering in the candlelight. Philip was right. There was no indication that anything had ever hung there.

My treasure hunt was a hollow thing, but I made myself go on with it. I would at least give a cursory glance to all the upper rooms; see what I owned.

The second flight of steps was narrower and darker. As I progressed upward my mind went back and I was once more counting gates. One—the gate at the bottom of the sea cliff; two—the picket gate facing the front of the house; three—the picket gate in the back yard leading to the drive; and four—the tall iron gate to the twisting road. That left three to find.

On the third floor all the doors opening off the long dark hall were welcomingly ajar, perhaps because they provided what little light there was. Just for a second I thought about Joanna's locked door and was glad I needn't open any of these rooms. I pushed the half-open door of the nearest room and it swung wide. The interior was dimly lighted through white lowered shades. I tugged on the dangling ring on a cord and the shade shot up, slapping loudly against the roller. Dust billowed, making me cough. I was in a smallish room, meagerly furnished with mismatched old furniture including a hideous chair constructed of leather and cattle horns. Philip could have the ancestor who had made that dreadful purchase.

Which brought me back to Philip—which brought

me back to the painting, which was not hanging here. I noted the brass bed dulled by dust and time, a chipped wicker chair, but no Joanna with her loving tender smile.

All the upper rooms were rather small; all adorned with tarnished gaslights curving gracefully from the walls. I wished they hadn't been removed from the downstairs. Even if these were inoperable they were a lovely bit of nostalgia. The faded wallpapers showed style changes and the rooms grew more neglected and more cluttered as I moved on down the dingy hall. I came at last to a room used for storage, guarded near the door by a wasp-waisted dress form. There were stacks of books, yellowed newspaper and magazines, tall dressers with dusty mirrors—and a trunk—my treasure chest at last.

I went down on my denim-clad knees before the humpbacked chest inlaid with etched and tarnished brass. It was a beauty in itself, but I was now eager to discover its secrets.

"Locked! Wouldn't you know!"

The padlock spelled the end of my adventure. I grabbed the infuriating thing and shook it; to no avail, of course.

I turned to the dressers, but they were empty except for dust curls and one small item, a jade unicorn on a broken chain. *It belongs to Joanna.* I don't know why I didn't consider that it could have easily belonged to mother or some other female member of the family. But I knew it was Joanna's.

The crunch of tires on gravel startled me from my reverie and I tucked the little pendant into my jeans pocket and went downstairs. I reached the back door just as Philip opened it to admit Elijah laden with a red ice chest proclaiming the virtues of a soft drink. He was followed by Erna with a sack held in the crook of her stringy arm.

"Milk," she announced.

Philip carried a bucket filled with cleaning supplies. He gave me a warm glance that turned my heart over in spite of any resolutions I had made to the contrary.

"Hi. You're walking very well today."

Erna took the bucket. "Now I can get down to brass tacks and get this place cleaned up right."

"Great," I said, then, hoping to find out if she could dig deep enough into that black pocket of hers to come up with the key to the treasure trunk I had found, I added, "Let's start on the third floor."

Philips' bronze-colored eyebrows shot up. "Oh, ho! Aren't you feeling frisky! As your doctor, I don't recommend heavy cleaning for you today."

Erna nodded briskly. "I work better alone anyway, and I've still got rooms down here to do. The lawyer paid me to have the house cleaned before you got here, but you went and jumped the gun on me. The third floor will be the last to be done," she said irrevocably. She grunted as she picked up the pail she had set down. "Best set to it."

Philip turned twinkling eyes to meet my blazing ones. "Better come for a drive with me. Nobody crosses Erna. You may as well get used to being bullied."

Elijah had been silently unloading milk and eggs into the ice chest, his lined brow set in a deep frown.

Erna said something that sounded like "Pah!" and took her pine-smelling bucket of water away. "You want me, I'll be in the music room. Don't intend to fix any lunch."

"She's downright insufferable sometimes," I fumed. "I didn't even know I had a music room. I should have made her show me the whole house that first afternoon." I had to grin a little sheepishly. "Of course I suppose she might have if I hadn't...." Deliberately, I left the sentence unfinished.

Elijah spoke now that Erna was gone. "Seven Gates is a mighty big house, bigger than it looks from the outside. Sixteen rooms, I think."

Philip grinned into my glowering face. "She means well, Erna does. Just blunt, forthright."

Elijah snorted.

I personally endorsed his unspoken comment, but I refrained from speaking my mind. I did need her and that was that.

Elijah turned toward the door. "I thought I'd trim up the front bushes—that is, unless you'd rather I started on the back." His benevolent old face cracked in a grin.

I had to laugh. "You start anywhere you like. I don't seem to have much control over what happens around here."

"Then I'd best set to it," he said in an excellent imitation of Erna.

We were all chuckling as the old man walked with his sideways gait out of the back door.

I walked into Philip's waiting arms at last.

"I thought they'd never go," he breathed into my hair.

We were quiet. It was enough to be together, touching, reaching out toward one another with our inner beings. My eyes were closed, my thoughts shut down until at last he spoke.

"I suppose we'd better go somewhere. Any place special?"

Reluctant to break the embrace, I cuddled closer, but the spell had been broken with words. I moved away saying, "I guess if we must go somewhere it might as well be a place called Wilde's. Do you know it? Elijah said I might be able to get a barometer like the one I broke."

"Wilde's?" he said with a slight pull of his mouth.

"You don't like him, either? Elijah recommended him but didn't want to take me there. Said he couldn't stand the man. What's wrong with him?"

"Not a thing, not a thing! Shall we go?"

"Shouldn't I change?"

"No, you look quite fetching. One would swear you had those jeans tailor-made, and the amber pattern in your shirt is exactly the color of your eyes. Those fantastic eyes!"

"I know. Just like Joanna's."

"I wouldn't know. I never had the pleasure."

And just like that it was back, the restraint between us.

"Lea, don't look like that. Come on, let's get out of here. I think I'm the one who should change." He glanced down at his long bare legs.

As he seemed determined to change at least the subject, I went along with him. "I don't see why you should. But what about your practice? What if you have a patient?"

"It's nice of you to worry about my poor practice. Are you afraid I . . . no, I'm getting ahead of myself. I fixed it up yesterday about my so-called practice."

He dug into a sweat-shirt pocket and produced what I thought was a small, flat camera. "My beeper. As long as we stay within fifty miles, I can be summoned—summarily. Come along, my darling. Wilde eagerly awaits you."

WILDE'S MARINE ANTIQUES was a real ship anchored in the first slip nearest the road at a big marina.

"While we're here, do you want to see Elijah's boat?"

"Oh, yes. I think Erna told me he still had his old fishing boat. Is it here, then?"

"There, down at the end. Come walk with me and we can see it better. I think the sun is going to make it out full force. There, I told you. What do you think of the *Golden Lady*?"

"Well, aside from the fact that she looks as old as her skipper, she's not as bad as I'd been led to believe. She's no beauty, but it looks as if she's in good repair."

"Oh, she's ready to take to sea anytime, I'm sure. But I understand she hasn't left the slip in thirty years or so."

"Makes you wonder why he hangs on to her."

Philip nodded reflectively. "He's had offers now and again, but he just glowers and stumps away. Expensive sentimentality, but if he can keep it up. . . ."

"Yes. Shall we try to find my barometer now?"

"Suppose there's no getting around it." He reminded me just a bit of his description of Elijah stumping away from offers for his *Golden Lady*.

I laughed and took his arm as we walked back along the grayed boards of the marina. "This Wilde must rely on a lot of tourist trade. There aren't that many people living close by."

"Are you kidding! Every woman within a hundred miles has at least one marine room. Except Erna. She shows remarkably good taste by studiously avoiding the man. I've seen her cross the street to keep out of his way several times."

"My, he certainly seems to get people's dander up. I thought you said there was nothing wrong with him."

He snorted. "There isn't. Not one damned thing!"

He helped me up the steep but plushly carpeted steps to the deck of the sleek ship. "This thing must have cost a fortune," I whispered.

"Pah!"

I giggled. "You sound like Erna. Now, be nice. Here comes the proprieter. Oh! I think I see what you mean!"

He was enough to take one's breath away, this man. He had pure silver hair in contrast to his deeply tanned skin and provocatively winged black brows. His eyes were black, so dark they appeared opaque, with a smudge of lashes any girl would have envied, yet they were aggressively masculine on him. He was tall, taller even than Philip, and put together as if by an artist. And the black eyes were bold.

"Good morning." He said it in a deep and resonant voice that added many beautiful things to the greeting.

Philip mumbled something, but I hadn't yet found my tongue. Wilde's eyes held me in their depths, promising the world and telling me beyond question that at that moment no other woman existed for him. All this in the time it takes to say "good morning," which I finally managed. This man was no stranger to me. I felt as if I had known him always.

I glanced at Philip. He looked more than ever like a college boy, his hands plucking idly at the frayed hem of his denim shorts. Perhaps he should have changed after all.

Wilde held out his hand, his smile radiating interesting lines from his eyes. Then, instead of the customary handshake he covered my unresisting hand with his left in a warm, intimate way. "John Wilde. And I need no introduction to you, Joannalea. I *may* call you Lea?"

I wanted to smile and say breezily, "Of course," but I was lucky to be able to nod dumbly.

"And you are even lovelier than I had heard."

The grapevine again, extending even beyond the village proper.

I retrieved my hand. This was ridiculous. I had never seen this man before, yet I had stood like this with him before. Déjà vu again. Or perhaps I had merely seen him in a dream; he was surely the kind of man young girls dream about. But I was no longer a young girl; I was a woman of twenty-three and I must stop this silly gaping.

"Thank you, Mr. Wilde."

"John," he corrected with his very personal smile.

"John," I acknowledged, smiling back until his bold eyes made a quick trip down my amber shirt and back to catch my gaze in the deep whirlpool of his.

Really! He is perfectly insufferable, I thought. Yet I couldn't help a secret smile as I took my gaze away and onto the merchandise displayed on the deck of the yacht. This man might sell antiques of the sea, as a very small sign claimed, but he sold John Wilde first and foremost. And I would have wagered that ninety percent of his female clientele bought one for the other. I couldn't guess his age; he might have been as young as thirty-five or a well-maintained fifty-five. And his casual half-unbuttoned silk shirt spelled wealth. John Wilde was not a man—he was a male phenomenon!

We completed my purchase so smoothly that I was surprised to find myself holding a wrapped parcel. I looked around for Philip.

"I believe you'll find your young man in the car. I'm afraid we. . . bored him."

I thought of poor Philip in his frayed shorts. "Oh, how dreadful of me to ignore the poor boy like that!" As soon as I said "poor boy" I regretted it, but it was too late.

"Poor boy indeed!" His white teeth gleamed as those hot dark eyes moved again, button by button, down my shirt. "I *shall* see you again." It was a statement, a promise and a dismissal, and called for no goodbye on my part.

I bumped into a diver's suit in my flustered haste to leave the ship. "Excuse me," I muttered to it, then blushed until my face burned red.

"Joanna—Lea." His voice caressed the one word into a beautiful two, and I risked a jerky wave in answer to his terribly graceful one.

The breeze that seemed to spring up about noon every day had blown away the thin overcast and now cooled my fiery cheeks. John was right about Philip's whereabouts. No doubt most of the male companions of Wilde's customers wound up waiting in the car.

Philip was gripping the steering wheel, staring

straight ahead as he let me get in the station wagon unassisted.

"Well?"

"I got it," I said and pointed unnecessarily to my package.

"The full treatment, no doubt!"

"Oh, at least! He is the most insufferable man! But undeniably gorgeous, nevertheless."

"I'd have thought, to hear you talk, you'd had enough of insufferable men." Philip's lips clamped hard on the words.

"Oh, Philip! Stop pouting! He's dreadful, okay?"

I scarcely thought him dreadful, but my saying so cheered Philip immensely, and he was his usual charming self as he drove us the few blocks to an oceanside restaurant for lunch. I did my best to attend to his conversation, but my mind kept slipping back to the feeling of déjà vu I had experienced with John.

It was two o'clock.

"I must get back to the office and wait for my nonexistent patients. Judy says it looks bad if I don't keep some semblance of office hours."

We gathered up our few belongings, left the restaurant and headed home.

"Philip, if you can't...well, make any money in that little town, why...?"

He swung me a quick look just as he turned the wagon into my drive. "I like it here." It was all he said.

"Of course. It's a pretty village. Thank you for taking me."

He nodded and gave me a brief salute before he drove away.

So much for tact, I thought. Poor Philip. I reflected as I entered the back door. Was it true I found insufferable men more exciting than. . . loving men? In spite of my discomfort with John Wilde I had to admit I had enjoyed the encounter. What Erna had said was true; I did attract men. I had always had quite a field of admirers to choose from, and I invariably chose the wrong ones. Was I like Joanna? Had she, too, chosen unwisely in the end, and had that choice led to her grisly murder?

I had to find out.

Grunting noises came from the dining room. Erna was polishing the table with such vigor she was out of breath.

"Erna, stop a minute."

She panted, "Glad to. Never could figure out how you got a great big table like this polished from one end to the other without the polish getting too dry."

"It looks beautiful. I want to ask you—is it really true about my aunt being the victim of. . . murder?"

She turned her attention and her cloth to the long mahogany sideboard. "What a thing to ask a body! Now this piece here. . . ."

"Erna!" I took her polish and held it childishly behind my back. "I think I have a right to know what happened to Joanna and in the house I live in. Please."

She stared at me thoughtfully from her cavernous eyes. "Seems funny *you* living in Seven Gates. I mean, it's like it's starting all over, you being so much alike and all. It's like the place still belongs to Joanna, God rest her soul, and like she only left it for a time. I catch myself thinking of you as her. Suppose it's what they call wishful thinking. Like that awful thing never happened to us."

I was tempted to tell her about my strange experiences when even I wasn't certain of my identity, but she would think me. . . what, insane? Or at least she'd label me overimaginative. I pulled away from my reflections. "Then Joanna *was* murdered?"

"Your mother never told you?"

"No."

She raised her head and began to speak in tones deep and fervent, her eyes glinting. "I'll tell you what you want to know and you'll wish you'd left it alone." She stood, hands pressed flat against the tabletop, eyes lifted, staring somewhere above her.

The artist in me longed for my brushes to capture this transformation and I shivered, partly with excitement about my subject, partly in fear of my Cassandra and her tale.

"It stormed that night, a freak storm in the middle of July. Joanna had spent weeks pacing the widow's walk at dusk. Then two or three nights of the week she would. . .disappear. I didn't know where she went, but I did know who she went to meet."

She paused and looked at me piercingly, and my flesh crept with revulsion, yet I felt an eerie awe of her. Her face, her speech, bore little resemblance to the bluff, forthright Erna Dwyer who cooked and cleaned and in her way fussed over me. What a painting she would make!

"Joanna didn't know I knew." She swept a triumphant glance over me, then went back to her story. "This night, this hot, close July night, she spent pacing the lookout room trying to see out the windows through the streams of water. It was a storm to end all storms, with lightning flashing and the thunder drowning out the crash of the surf on the cliff. But I knew, and she should have known—'' here her voice registered contempt ''—that he couldn't come from the sea or the cliff that night. If you—if she had been in her right mind she would have known she would see him from the kitchen window—as I did.''

Her sudden malicious laughter chilled me. ''Erna....'' I started, but her words rolled brutally over mine, her eyes boring into my face.

''She never saw him. Finally she went to her room.'' Her leathery forehead puckered. ''We were alone in the house, Joanna and me. Her sister was married by then and the parents dead. The Brandts always die young. Even the old captain wasn't really old; he was only the first.''

''Go on,'' I prompted, wanting to get off the subject of my family's early demises.

''Then somebody split her head open with an ax—a hatchet,'' she said baldly. ''But it was always referred to as the ax murder.''

My hands shook and I had the uncontrollable urge to look over my shoulder. ''Who...'' I croaked.

She had come out of her trance or transformation—whatever it was. She spread her hands, flapping them in her usual crowlike manner. ''They never found out.''

''But the man you saw....''

''He didn't do it!'' She spat the words. ''And anyway, I was the only one who knew about him.''

''And you never told.''

''I never told.''

I let out my breath and held up the polish. ''Thank you for telling me. I had to know.''

She snatched the bottle with her yellowed hand. ''Don't thank me! Before long you'll wish you'd never dredged it up.''

She turned to her polishing with a vengeance, her long scrawny neck arched oddly upward, and I marveled that a few moments ago she had possessed that strange weird beauty. . . the same kind of beauty as that of the dead twisted trees that clung to the lonely wind-carved cliff Seven Gates was built upon. I *would* paint her, and I had to start now before the vision was lost. I ran up the stairs to begin.

HOURS HAD PASSED before I heard Erna's querulous voice from the door of the telescope room.

''Supper's been ready for an hour. I called and called. You artists!''

I stared. She was neither vulture nor Cassandra. She was just an old woman, mundane, complaining.

''Better come down before it's completely dried out.''

I quickly turned the wet painting toward the wall without looking at it. I had done it in a fever of excitement and I was afraid to see what I had done. I felt it would be good, by far the best thing I had ever done, but I wasn't ready to judge it. I would see what I had done to Erna later. I followed her down to dinner.

CHAPTER SEVEN

SUMMER had returned to the coast with brilliant sunshine and a warm eastern breeze after four days of chilly overcast. I had sent my assignment of cards off to Chicago and felt I had earned a lazy day. The constraint between Phillip and me had abated and we had spent two out of the three preceding evenings before a crackling fire in the front room acquainting each other with our past lives, though I thought both of us shied away from a lot of family talk. Of course I had no relatives to speak of, and perhaps it was the same with him. This morning I was content to wander slowly in the ruins of the back garden.

Gangly unpruned roses grew tall among the weeds that Elijah hadn't attacked yet. What had once been lawn with a rose border on three sides was now patchy, spreading sandburs, festooned with still-tender fuzzy green balls. A tall pine tree reared upward into the gloriously blue sky, coating its deep shadow with a bed of brown needles that crunched softly beneath my feet. My sandaled toe struck an object that I unburied. It was a small plastic doll, headless and pinkly naked. My mother's? Or Joanna's?

I sat down in the deep shade, mindless of the thick coating of dust. The pine mingled with the salt smell of the ocean, the drift of fragrance from some distant flower. I closed my eyes, both hands cupping the little doll, a remnant from the past. I let my mind drift where it willed.

There had been a swing; I had seen the rope scar on a sloping limb above. I fancied I could hear childish voices.

"Push me! Push me!"

Joanna pumped, leaning far back, her black braids dragging on the worn dirt scooped into a hollow under the board swing. "I can go higher—higher than the sky!" Her sturdy legs strained to achieve the greatest height ever.

"Joanna! You'll go too high! You'll go right over upside down!"

"High! Higher than the sky!" Joanna screamed in exhilaration. And exhilaration coursed like a drug through my veins.

"Oh, please, Joanna! Don't!"

"Oh, all right, you little scaredy-cat!" I dragged my feet, scuffing up great clouds of dust, slowing, slowing. I said, "Then give me my doll, scaredy-cat!"

"No! You said I could play with her all day."

"Well, I changed my mind. Give it here!"

A tremulous wail quivered through the pine rustle.

"Now look what you did! You broke her head right off, mean old Joanna!"

"Well," I said, "it was my doll, and if I want to break its old head off, I can!"

A little cry soughed away on the breeze. I blinked and shook my head. I glanced down at my hands. They were clenched and empty. The headless doll lay six feet away, half-buried in the pine needles.

Footsteps made me jump.

Philip crouched down beside me. "I didn't mean to startle you. Were you daydreaming?"

"I must have been." Was that what it was, a dream? It had seemed so real, dreadfully real.

I looked away from Philip's smiling, inquiring eyes. "I was daydreaming about what it would have been like to have been Joanna—or mother—when they were children." When said aloud it was simple. "For a little while I *was* Joanna, swinging higher than the sky. It was wonderful!"

I moved into the sun and covered the doll with a blanket of pine needles and a small pine cone. I said, "It's better to bury the past."

Philip looked at me quickly. "I totally agree, but that is quite a switch for a girl who was just playing Joanna."

"My mother used to say that. Bury the past."

"Well, I'm sure she was right." He put his arm around my shoulders. "Still, I'm glad you had fun swinging."

I looked intently at my shoes as I said, "What if I told you I also had fun breaking my doll?"

He grabbed me by the arms, pulling me up and giving me a little shake. "I'd say it's a damned good thing I came along to wake you out of that daydream! Really, Lea, fantasizing is one thing, but acting it out puts it in a different category."

"Oh, it wasn't all fantasy." I uncovered the broken doll with my shoe. "You'll notice I gave her a decent burial—with a monument."

He let go of me. "You didn't. . . ."

"Tear her head off? No, I found her that way."

Philip picked up the toy and handed it to me. He watched me closely as he said, "Sometimes you scare me, Lea. Your streak of drama, if that's what it is, is uncanny. Do all artists come that way?"

I laughed, tossing off the daydream. "No, I don't think so. Anyway, don't take it all so seriously. It's nothing. As you say, my 'streak of drama.'" Then I told him about running into the car while daydreaming on the way home from school. But I kept to myself the fantasy on the widow's walk when I nearly fell.

"Well, I think," he said, "that it's time you stopped that sort of thing. You're going to get yourself killed."

I stopped, sick, the pain in my head unbearable, splitting. My fingers flew to my head.

"Lea! What is it?"

"Migraine, I think. Or perhaps not; it's going away, thank goodness! I couldn't bear to go through what my poor mother did. What can I do?"

"You're sure it's gone?"

"Completely. Strange, that's the second one. No, the third. In fact, I meant to ask you about them, but I forgot."

He turned to me to look at him. "Lea, I would like you to see another doctor. There's a good one in Silver City. Do you trust me to make an appointment with him for you? Much as I need the patients, I'm afraid I can't be objective with you."

"Please do make the appointment."

"Good, that's settled." He drew me close and his mouth sought mine in little brushing kisses that lighted leaping fires inside me. I clung to his hard muscular body.

Erna was pouring coffee when we walked into the dining room. "About time! I was. . . ." She stared and the cup she held fell to the floor and shattered, the dark liquid spreading in a puddle on the carpet.

"What?" My eyes followed her gaze. She gaped, white lipped, at the doll I still held.

Her shaking finger pointed. "Where do you get that?" she shouted, her deep eyes widened.

Shaken, I dropped the toy.

"This?" asked Philip calmly as he retrieved it. "We found it under the pine tree. Why?"

I spoke without thinking. "It was Joanna's, wasn't it?"

"It was," she agreed solemnly.

Philip shrugged. "So what?"

Erna kneeled and started picking up the shards of the thin china cup, her agitation evident in the fact that she ignored the spreading stain on the Oriental carpet.

"How can you be sure whose it was? It must be very old," Philip insisted.

"I gave it to her. I remember, all right," she stated flatly, then with a start whipped off her print apron and dabbed ineffectively at the wet spot.

Suddenly I wanted to put my arms around her spare old body and cry, for Joanna hadn't cared about the doll at all. I took a step toward her, then stopped myself. How foolish! How did I know how Joanna had felt about the little gift from her poorer friend? I *had* to stop these fancies. Philip was right.

I said, "I am sorry. I can understand that it would be a shock having it turn up after all these years."

She finished her mopping. "Be hard to get that stain out. I had no call to go dropping that cup. I'll pay for it, but I doubt if it can be replaced. It's funny, that's all, her things turning up after all this time. Gave me a fright. Can't think why."

"Things? Plural?" asked Philip.

Erna lowered her chin into her black collar. "Better eat. It's getting cold."

"I know. What else has 'turned up,' as you say, that belonged to Joanna?"

"I suppose she means the hatchet," I said, drawing a shuddering breath.

"A what!"

"Hatchet. Buried in the kitchen table. Elijah mended it."

"Good Lord! Wasn't your aunt...?"

"Murdered? Yes, with just such an instrument."

"Let's eat," Erna injected harshly.

"But...."

"Let's eat!"

And that's what we did, silently.

PHILIP PUSHED HIS CHAIR back from the table. "I think it is high time I met the elusive Joanna!"

Erna dropped her fork.

I nearly laughed at the openmouthed expression on her face. "He means her portrait. In fact, I've been meaning to ask you about that. It seems to...well, I saw it at the head of the stairs."

"You couldn't! It's in her room!"

"Well," I insisted stubbornly, "it wasn't. I know it wasn't on the landing when I first went up the stairs, then I saw it there and then it was gone. I thought it might have been taken out to be cleaned or something."

"I never touched it!" She stared back and forth between Philip and me as if one of us had to tell her the answer to the puzzle. I had never seriously believed that she'd had anything to do with its disappearance; now I was convinced of it.

"Maybe Elijah moved it," I suggested.

"Could be. Don't see why he'd be moving it around. Sure you saw it there?"

"I saw it, I tell you!"

"Well, no use getting hysterical about it. Probably a good explanation...." She left the sentence unfinished and began to clear the table.

Philip stood up. "Well, let's hunt it down, starting with where it's supposed to be."

Erna's glance locked with mine for an instant, then I quickly looked away. I had the feeling that she did, also.

Philip continued, "Shall we go, ladies? In search of Joanna?"

Erna started picking up dishes. "You two go. I have dishes to wash."

My instinct was to dodge the issue by offering to help, but Philip was insistently holding out his hand to help me up. "The key," I said. "I don't have the key."

"It's on your bureau. I found it on the floor after...." She disappeared into the kitchen.

I hung back, following Philip up the stairs. At the top he stopped, his eyes roaming the place where I had said the painting had hung—where it *had* hung!

"I *know* there's no sign of any painting ever hanging there. You don't have to remind me!"

"I wasn't going to. What did it look like?"

"Oh, it's large, at least three by four feet, in a fancy gilt frame. It looks quite heavy; that's why I never suspected Ollie and Mark of playing a prank with it. Not that they absolutely couldn't—they are an ingenious pair—but it wouldn't be easy and I *was* in the house when it disappeared."

"No," he murmured, running his hands over the wallpaper. "It wouldn't have been easy. I'm sure it wasn't the boys."

"Then you do believe me finally?" I asked sharply.

There was a slight hesitation before his answer that emptied it of meaning for me. "Yes. Now let's find the damned thing. Incidentally, are all the rooms kept locked?"

"No, only Joanna's."

He wondered why with his eyebrows, then shrugged.

"I assume the door's locked. I imagine Erna relocked it after... I was in there."

"Oh, then you saw the portrait there."

My voice was heavy with my settling depression. "No, Philip, I did not. I was struck with my first headache just as I entered the room. I wasn't noticing paintings."

"Still, subconsciously you might have."

"Let's drop it. I really think I'd like to rest."

"No, let's not drop it. Let's get this over with. I won't have it hanging over us like this. I want this... mystery cleared up."

He accompanied me to the telescope room.

"Nice view," he commented, looking out through the French doors. "Treacherous-looking railing, though. Better stay far back from that thing!"

Now was the time to tell him how I had nearly fallen from there that strange night, but I kept silent. I suspected he had doubts about my mental state as it was. I longed to confide that I was frightened, fling myself into his arms and lose myself and my fears in his kisses, but something held me back. I had trusted men before and I knew where that got me. I handed him the key.

"Which room?"

"Right there." I pointed to the door just like all the doors off that hall, but to me it was set apart by memories of intense, unbearable pain. Again I hung back.

Philip fitted the key into the big square lock and swung open the door. "Coming?"

I took two steps after him, but when he was inside I stopped again. "Is. . . is it in there?"

"I don't see it, but I do see where it used to hang. You can see where the wallpaper isn't faded. Well, I guess *you* can't. Lea, are you afraid to come in?"

I laughed sheepishly, but still I didn't move. "In a way I am. I suppose I associate the room with pain."

"Well, you needn't come in. No reason to, and in time you'll get over the dread without forcing yourself to do something that frightens you. I'm going to make sure you get a good going-over by Dr. Smithers—and soon. I can't have my girl getting sick, now can I?"

If he hadn't still been just inside that room, I'd have flung myself all over him when he said, "My girl." I was suffused with happiness and when I spoke I suspected it was evident in my tone, though my words were mundane enough.

"No, it would make you look bad as a doctor, wouldn't it, even if you have rejected me as a patient."

"It would indeed. Must keep up my image, above

all. Seriously, I'll have Judy phone Silver City as soon as I get back to the office."

Judy, I thought.

"Now what's the matter? I've never seen anyone register such changing emotions. You do not have a poker face, my darling. What is it?" He propelled me toward the staircase.

"Oh, nothing, really."

"Come, come. You might as well tell me."

"Well, I thought... that is, I could call that doctor myself from the village. I don't need *Judy*." In spite of myself I leaned too hard on the last word.

"Ah! Do I detect the little green monster shining in those wondrous eyes?" he said, taking the final step in front of me.

He tipped up my chin, and I set my mouth against the flush beginning at my throat. "Well, she does seem to have designs on her employer."

"Does she now? And you're jealous."

I wouldn't meet his eyes, staring instead at the one wayward lock of gold brown hair that fell over his forehead. "And it ill becomes me," I quoted.

"Oh, I don't know. I think the green sparks in your eyes and the rosy blush on your cheeks are charming. Honestly, though, I've always felt jealousy had an undeservedly bad name. I think every emotion has its value... as well as its proper magnitude, of course."

His arms were reassuringly strong when he pulled me to him, and I mumbled against his neck, "My, aren't you wise today."

"Only every other Friday." He kissed me, then groaned, "Damn the office hours!"

When he had left I sat down on the bottom step,

hugging my happiness to my bosom. Philip loved me and I could feel the smile on my face. Wherever Joanna's portrait was, let it stay. It was of the least importance in my life now that I had my own love. Just at that moment I thought I would die if I lost him. . . .

"Well?"

I jumped up, startled.

Erna was wiping her hands on a fresh print apron.

"Oh, the painting! It wasn't there."

"It can't be gone!" She wagged her head disbelievingly. "It can't have just got up and walked off."

"No, and you might as well know there's no nail or hole in the wall where I saw it hung, either."

"Then you imagined it."

"I didn't. I saw it. She was wearing. . . ."

"I know what she was wearing and you probably remembered the portrait from when you were in Joanna's room."

"Well, in any case it's gone. Elijah must have taken it away to have it cleaned. We'd better ask him. I'm sure he meant it as a surprise."

"*You* ask him. Meanwhile we'd best look for it in the house. It could just be. . . ." She didn't finish the sentence, but started up the stairs. "Might as well start at the top and work down."

"Oh, I already searched the third floor, and I've meant to ask—there's a trunk up there in the farthest room. Do you know where the key is? It's padlocked."

She stopped on the stairs and turned to give me a piercing look. "That's Joanna's trunk," she said, as if that were answer enough.

I let it go. One problem at a time was sufficient.

First we had to find Joanna—later would do to open her trunk.

We searched the second story, turning out closets of clothing from decades before, looking under beds that ranged from one that might have been a John Belter, so exquisitely was it carved, to a honey-blond affair from the post-World War II era. We ended in the music room, hideously decorated with more of the light wood, only the ornate walnut grand piano having a vestige of dignity.

I slumped onto the piano bench. "It's too big to hide easily. If it were in the house we would have found it."

Erna glared around her, her fists on her hips. "That just beats all. Must be Elijah's got it, after all."

"Yes, I hope so. I hate to think it might have been stolen. It's a very good painting. I wonder why I haven't heard of the artist. He certainly deserves recognition."

Erna was staring out the bay window where the piano stood. "Didn't have much chance. He drowned right out there. I never did care much for sailboats, for all they look pretty. They found the boat, but Jay Savage. . . ."

"Pity," I said, but my mind had edged over. Savage—Wilde. I wondered if I would see John Wilde again. Then I realized that Erna was still talking.

"He was tall and slim, never seemed to get enough to eat, or have any money, either. Most folks didn't appreciate how good he was."

There was a vehemence in her tone that made me glance at her, then look quickly away. It seemed she still felt his death keenly.

"When did the accident happen?" I asked, to fill in

the painful silence that ensued after Erna had clamped her mouth shut after her last word.

Her eyes flashed and died. "Don't matter. He's dead and gone before he even had his chance."

"Couldn't he have escaped? They only found the boat, you said."

"No," she said flatly, and turned a set face toward me. "Leave him alone. It's all done and past. Leave it alone!" This last was flung over her shoulder as her stiff back disappeared into the gloom of the hall.

CHAPTER EIGHT

I COULDN'T leave it alone, of course.

I had been overcome with a pervading sadness as I left the music room and went upstairs. It would have been funny to some to imagine Joanna and Erna in love with the same man, for I knew that's what had occurred. I felt it in my bones, as my mother might have said. I felt it in my bones, too, that Joanna had meant something in John Wilde's life, also. But I was sure that as exciting as John was, it wasn't he who had been Joanna's final love.

No, that special dreamy smile had been awakened by the artist who had captured it on the canvas that was now missing. I had to find it; I didn't question the urgency of my conviction. Jay Savage's work had to be preserved, and if there were deeper, more confusing feelings bound up in the quest, then I would let them lie.

I let my hair blow free in the wind on the widow's walk while I looked with new eyes on the malevolent undulations of the ocean as the sun scuttled behind a cloud. "I'll find that painting. I'll keep you alive, Jay Savage, if it's the last thing I do."

The tide had turned and an angry wave lashed at the cliff. I shuddered. No, Erna was right. The sea had claimed its victim. I fled from the sound and the fine salt spray.

ERNA WAS FLOURING a board. "Noodles," she said by way of explanation.

"Sounds good. Do you have an idea where I might find Elijah?"

"Cemetery, I'd guess."

"Is that far?"

"No, not very. You go up the road toward town. It's, oh, a quarter of a mile or so. Hard to see from the road. There's a narrow road turns off into it. Supper should be ready by the time you get back. Chicken and homemade noodles if I get started on them." She rolled up her sleeves and moved to the pantry.

I set off up the gravel drive and passed through what I had termed the fourth gate that gave onto the road. The turnoff was exactly as Erna had described it, and in a car I would have missed it. Thick trees intertwined over a narrow, weedgrown tire track. There wasn't much traffic into the cemetery, I observed. A short walk under the tunnel of trees brought me to an open iron gate, a twin to the one leading to Seven Gates. Could this have once been part of the old captain's holdings? Perhaps he had donated this portion, or sold it off. At any rate, I was willing to bet I had found the fifth gate. That left just two more to go.

The cemetery was a lovely, peaceful place: lush green grass, old-fashioned monuments adorned with fanciful angels and flowing carved vines and flowers. Small trees cast long afternoon shadows and roses lined the cobblestone track that meandered through the stones. I saw Elijah on the far side trimming around a tall white monument of classic design. To follow the path would take me far out of my way, so with some slight misgivings I stepped onto the grass and threaded my way among the graves, stopping now and then to read a line of poetry or of praise in memory of someone's passing. As I came closer to Elijah I saw that he had sat back on his heels, shears still, his face turned toward the sun.

He didn't hear me as I came close, though I was within his peripheral vision, I thought. He was seemingly lost in a world of his own. I was loath to disturb him, and to pass the moments before I must, I glanced at the name on the monument.

Joanna Brandt.

My heart lurched, then sank, as her dreamy face floated before me. In a moment or two I had put my tangled thoughts into perspective. Why should it surprise me, shock me, to come upon Joanna's grave? I knew she was dead, and where else would she have been buried? But I wasn't comfortable standing over Joanna's last resting place. I wasn't comfortable with death, even when it was old, dead history. There was no use trying to pretend I didn't have some silly childish fears about it.

Elijah still hadn't noticed me. "Elijah?" I said softly.

He turned slowly. "It's you," he said, not in the rusty old voice I knew, but in a soft, barely audible murmur.

Falling in with the hush of the place, I almost whispered, "Erna told me where I might find you. I. . . well, I was wondering if you took the painting."

"Eh?" His strange, different-colored eyes opened up and he shook his head. "The painting? What painting are you talking about?" he rasped in his normal voice.

"Joanna's. The portrait is missing. I thought you must have. . . ."

His knees cracked as he suddenly stood up. "Those goldurned boys! Well, I won't hold still for this. No, sir! That is a valuable picture. I'm going to get the constable!" He took two steps, then turned. "You sure it's gone?"

"Well, Erna hasn't done anything with it, and I don't see how the kids. . . ."

"Can't be anybody else," he declared. "Don't know what they'd want with it, though. I'll just come along and have a look around for it. It must be there."

"But we've looked everywhere!"

"I suppose you looked where it's always been—in her room?"

"Of course. It isn't there, I tell you!" I folded my lips against the irritation. Nobody would take my word for anything. I clumped angrily along behind him, then mentally shrugged my shoulders. If he wanted to waste his time, it was certainly up to him. I watched with amusement his peculiar windblown gait and grinned as he grumbled all the way back to the house.

"Blinkin' rascals probably think it's funny, stealing things. 'Course, not for a minute do I think it isn't in the house somewhere. But it's just like them no-good brats. No upbringing at all!"

He banged the back screen door unceremoniously and clumped up the stairs. Erna was not in the kitchen, though her cut noodles were, apparently ready to add to a steaming aromatic kettle on the stove. I took a quick peek at the simmering chicken and tested it for doneness, then I followed in Elijah's noisy wake to Joanna's room.

The door was open. My breathing quickened and my steps lagged, then I went to stand in the doorway. "Well, are you satisfied that it's really gone?"

"Gone! It's hanging right there where it's always been. Big as life!"

I rushed into the room and stared. Over the limed oak mantle hung the portrait, smiling, amber-clad, and mocking by its very presence.

"But Philip. . . ." I stopped. Philip wouldn't lie to me! But how could he explain this? I backed out of that awful room, my head swimming, throbbing. "I must have misunderstood. I—I thought. . . I saw it at the head of the stairs. I saw. . . ." I forced myself to order my speech. It would do no good to have Elijah thinking worse of my mental powers than he already must. "I'm sorry I disturbed you."

But he wouldn't let it go. "Nothing's ever hung at the head of the stairs. You must have imagined it." His eyes sharpened. "Headache again?"

I nodded. "I have some pills."

He put a great arm around me and walked me to my room. "You take your pills and don't you let anybody put anything over on you."

He smelled of new-cut grass and fresh air, and I would have liked to bury my face against his grandfatherly chest, but he gave my shoulders a little squeeze and let me go.

"Lie down now and take your medicine. Old Eli'll let the crone downstairs know you'll be a little while. You take good care of my girl, you hear?"

I nodded again and we parted at my door.

When I had taken the medication and the throbbing had subsided, I thought affectionately of the old man. He was a dear, good friend. My mind skipped to Philip. He *wouldn't* lie to me about the missing portrait's being in Joanna's room. It was too easily checked, for one thing. Besides, I could think of no reason, no matter how farfetched, for him to do so. In fact, it made no sense that the portrait should be disappearing and turning up in these mysterious ways. Someone was deliberately trying to upset me. But who had anything to gain by it? Reluctantly my mind fastened on Erna, yet I was sure she hadn't had the opportunity somehow to put the painting in the upper landing. Of course, she had the keys.

And Philip had the key to Joanna's room! With a sinking heart I remembered he hadn't returned it to me after he had come out of the room.

"No, he wouldn't lie to me. He wouldn't!" Tears rushed to my eyes, but I willed them back.

"SUPPER!" ERNA'S VOICE was raucous with the volume she used to call up the stairs.

She was quiet as she ladled out the savòry dinner. The noodles were delicious and I told her so, but constraint hung heavy over the table. Finally she broke a long silence. "I hear Joanna's back."

"Maybe she was never gone."

"Doc wouldn't lie! If he said that picture wasn't there, it wasn't there!"

I sighed wearily. "I know. I don't really believe Philip lied about it. I wonder if it *could* possibly be Ollie and Mark playing tricks?"

"Hah! You trying to tell me they sneaked in with a picture bigger than they are, got the key from—where is it, by the way?"

"I. . . I'm not sure." I wouldn't tell her Philip had it! "But the boys wouldn't be concerned about that key. They're very enterprising, those two. I suppose it's just barely conceivable they're doing these things. Just barely."

"Hmmph! I don't like it! It's enough to give a body the heebie-jeebies. Still, things always did go on around here. Joanna was behind most of 'em. Teased your mother something fearful sometimes. Used to hide her things, when Leanna demanded to know what she'd done with them, she'd say in a ghosty kind of voice, 'Look beyond the seventh gate.' She always gave Leanna her things back in the end. But my, how her eyes would shine when she thought she had you! Well, that's all over and has been." She let out a heavy breath and started gathering up the dishes.

The skin prickled at the nape of my neck. "Beyond the seventh gate. Erna, do you think. . . ?" What had I been going to say? I decided not to risk making a bigger fool of myself than I had. I would put that story away in the back of my mind and take it out and examine it later. "Is there any dessert?"

"Fruit. Don't want to make you fat. You going to talk to those boys and their mamas?"

"I believe I'd better."

That was where we left it. Erna washed the dishes and I dried them in a strained silence. The pain pills made me drowsy early and I took myself off to bed before it was completely dark.

Philip hadn't lied. It must be the boys. It couldn't be. . .no, I refused to think about my aunt. But my dreams were clouded with images of gates and a smiling, mocking Joanna.

CHAPTER NINE

THE NEXT afternoon I had set up my easel, but I hadn't unpacked my paints. Philip was sprawled on a plaid blanket chewing on the stem of a foxtail, Erna's wicker basket beside him on the beige sand.

"If you're not going to paint, why don't you join me? I make a tolerable pillow."

I turned from the shimmering, sun-dancing water. He looked lazy and content. I didn't want to share my disturbed thoughts with him.

"Come on. There's something on your mind. Can't you tell me?" He held out his arms and I stretched myself out beside him in the sun.

"Philip, she's back," I said tensely. "The painting is hanging in Joanna's room. Elijah made me look. It's really there."

He sat up with a jerk. "Are you kidding? Well, it wasn't there when I looked. You saw it!"

I worried the cuticle on my thumbnail. "No, I didn't. Remember, I didn't go in?"

"Well, surely you believe me!" There was a pause. "Oh, I see."

"Did you believe me, really, when I said it was hanging at the landing?"

"And there was no nail. Yes, I see. I confess I thought you had imagined it." He was quiet for a moment, then he lay back down and settled me against his shoulder. "Is that all that was bothering you? Not that that's not plenty."

I loathed having to go on, but I knew I must. My voice was unnaturally high as I asked, "The key—what did you do with Joanna's key?"

"Key?"

"You didn't give it back. Oh, Philip, please understand that I do trust you. It's just that I've got to start getting some of this cleared up or it's going to drive me out of my mind. You don't know! That awful hatchet, and thinking I was going insane when that portrait . . . and such peculiar things happening."

"Hey, hey! Calm down. I think something's happened, more than the portrait. What is it?"

"No, not really," I lied. I had tried to keep Erna's tale about Joanna's jokes out of my head, but it wavered there in my brain like a dark cloud hanging over me.

"Well, if you won't tell me, I can't make you, but I know you're keeping something from me, and have been. It's strange how well I feel I know you—it's only been ten days. I keep giving myself these scientific little lectures—that it's too soon to be in love—but I just can't be scientific about you, my darling."

He didn't kiss me with his lips but with his sun-flecked eyes, and I felt as if my body would melt with love for him. In shaky words I told him, "And I keep giving myself unscientific lectures about how I can be so lucky—when I know how love has always been so unlucky for me."

"Not this time. I'd die, I think, before I'd willingly hurt you." Tenderly he cupped my cheek in his hand and pressed his sun-hot lips to my temple.

The tears I hadn't shed since I was a little girl,

hadn't been able to shed for my mother, welled up in my eyes and slid down my cheeks. Philip kissed them away, murmuring, "My precious, I'll never let anything happen to you, never."

We lay pressed close together, lost in the oneness of our bodies for a long time. When we sat up it was some time before either of us spoke.

Finally I said quietly, "The sun is getting low."

He picked up my sweater and laid it across my shoulders. "Shall I open the wine?"

"Please."

He took the corkscrew to the ruby bottle and I laid out the ironstone plates Erna had packed. "Crystal glasses," I noted. "Erna's surpassing herself on our lunch."

"Most romantic. I wouldn't have believed it of her. Do you think she's encouraging us, Lea? She doesn't look like she's got a romantic bone in her body."

I nibbled on a sandwich. "The crusts cut off and linen napkins. It would appear that she might be playing Cupid. I wonder why? You're wrong about her, though; I think she was once deeply in love—and deeply hurt by it."

"Erna!"

"Erna. Why not?"

"She could never have been a beauty."

"No, and Joanna was."

Philip groaned. "Let's forget about Joanna. Who was Erna's lover, do you think—if indeed she had one, which I still doubt."

I stuck out my tongue at him. "I'm not prepared to supply this little town with any more gossip," I said. "Anyway, maybe rather than matchmaking she's just trying to keep us occupied and out of the house. She's as possessive about the place as if it were her own."

"Ah! Could it be she thinks it ought to be? Oh, I'm grasping at straws. Erna's as honest as the day is long."

I shivered a little. "Believe me, I hope so. She scares me sometimes."

Philip poured a second glass of wine, then held up the cut crystal, turning it slowly. The wine-tinted prisms glittered and made colored patterns of reflected light on my cream-colored slacks.

"What exactly scares you about her?"

"Well," I began, "for one thing she told me about Joanna's murder—no, it wasn't that. It's the way she tells things. So . . . well, she gets what I think of as her Cassandra, prophetess-of-doom look and her voice gets so fervent."

"Go on."

"I guess what's really got me going is what she said at dinner last night." I told him then of Joanna's pranks or little jokes.

"Look for them beyond the seventh gate," he repeated slowly, his smooth golden forehead puckered into two vertical lines between his brows. "You have an obsession with those gates."

"Then so did Joanna!" I flared.

"Hush. Lie down beside me." He pulled me down to his shoulder once more. "I may be hearing something different from what you're telling me. You don't even half believe it's Joanna's ghost come back to play hide-and-seek with the family heirlooms, do you?"

I bit back the retort that I didn't consider a murder

weapon to be an heirloom; I knew he was only thinking about the portrait.

"No, though my young friends, Ollie and Mark told me there was a ghost. What does the village grapevine have to say about that?"

He'd found his foxtail again and twirled it in his fingers. "Well, there's not much to talk about in a small town besides each other. There have been rumors of a ghost ever since the tragedy, I understand. Even the town constable claims the dubious distinction of having seen her. But that's only after hoisting a few around the stove on a rainy winter's night, I believe. It wouldn't be natural if there *weren't* a ghost story. An old mysterious house with a mystic name, an unsolved murder of a beautiful woman. It's nothing more than stories, Lea."

"I know, but one can't help but be nervous."

"I wonder if you shouldn't leave the house. You know I don't want you going back to Chicago, but maybe you should move, at least until you're feeling stronger. After all, you *have* gone through a lot."

It was tempting to put the house behind me with all its mysteries. Yet I already loved it and I had made countless plans for it. I would move all that awful yellow furniture out of the music room, for instance. There were enough really good pieces of walnut scattered her and there on all three stories to make the lower floor quite lovely. Of course, I could do all this in the daytime and sleep somewhere else. That is, I could if I had enough money. And I didn't.

"No, I'm really all right there. Erna's okay. I don't honestly suspect her of any shenanigans. I confess I would feel better if they had caught the murderer those twenty-odd years ago, but it's foolish to think he'd be hanging around waiting for a second victim."

"They never even had a suspicion of who might have done it?"

"I don't think so. Of course, I really don't know any more about it than what Erna and the boys have told me. Mother never mentioned it once. She wouldn't have. Erna withheld evidence, though; that I do know."

His eyes questioned me.

"Yes. According to her she saw a man on the grounds that night, but she never told. She claims to be certain that he couldn't or wouldn't have done it."

"That's Erna, all right. I wonder what the motive was. Why would anyone kill Joanna?" he mused.

"It was a crime of passion," I said.

"Oh, you've looked into it, then?"

My eyes flew open in surprise. "Why, no. I guess I just assume so. She was a passionate woman." I laughed. "Well, I suppose I assume that, too, because how would I really know for sure?"

But I did know—that was the disturbing thing.

Philip chuckled as he helped gather the picnic left-overs. "Let's leave the basket here and have that look around for your sixth gate you're so keen on locating. I confess I don't worry about *that* preoccupation of yours, though I'm not so hot on your obsession with your aunt. By the way, did you know that obsession can mean possession by evil spirits?"

He was busy shaking out the blanket so that he didn't see the way his words hit me, like a hammer-blow to my solar plexus. It was only momentary, but it left me weak and frightened. I flashed back to the night on the widow's walk. Had I been in possession of myself when I was called nearly to my death by that voice from the sea? I pushed my hands hard to my head, as if trying to squeeze out such thoughts.

Philip gently laid his hands over mine. "What is it?"

I had shut my eyes, and when I opened them I saw his face taut with anguish. "Oh, Philip, I'm sorry. I didn't mean to worry you."

"Is it a headache?"

I shook my head. "It's nothing, really. A goose walking over my grave, I guess. Let's get after that sixth gate, shall we? That is, if I can count the one at the cemetery." I made an effort to still the quaking of my knees, and after a few steps the fear Philip's innocent words had instilled in me began to dissipate.

"As it happens, you can count it. I checked. It was given to the community more than a hundred years ago by the old captain's widow when he died—ashore, by the way."

I was forgetting my queerness of a few moments ago and I said excitedly, "I just knew it! So that leaves only two to find. It would help if I knew the old boundaries."

He smirked and told me, "Well, chicken, it just so happens I know. Playing chess with the only lawyer in town has its advantages. So suppose you allow me to walk the boundaries with you, then we'll come back and finish the wine."

As we walked toward a stand of trees to the south of the property Philip began to recite:

"Up from Earth's Centre through the Seventh Gate
I rose, and on the Throne of Saturn sate,
And many a knot unravel'd by the Road;
But not the Master-knot of Human Fate

There was the Door to which I found no Key;
There was the Veil through which I might not see."

He paused.

"That's from the *Rubaiyat* of Omar Khayyam! Omar, the tentmaker. . . . Of course! That's what the old captain named Seven Gates for! I haven't thought of those verses since school. You're a very clever fellow, you know, to have remembered it." I resisted mulling over any possible mystic significance the old words might cast on the recent events in my life and chattered on. "If he simply liked the poetry, my ancestor was probably not referring to any real seven gates at all. Still, it will be fun searching. There is more to that verse, but I can't quite recall it.

"Some little talk awhile of me and thee
There was—and then no more of thee and me."

Philip took my hand as we walked. "That verse is too likely to start that goose walking again. But I have to confess I didn't remember the poem, at least not to impress you by reciting it from memory. I looked it up last night. Seven Gates had rung a bell in my head and I finally recalled what it reminded me of. It seems the old captain was as fanciful as his beautiful, many-greated granddaughter."

I threw off the last of my apprehensions; I was a modern, educated woman, not a superstitious sixteenth-century peasant girl after all. "Well, I still think you're clever, even if you did just learn it last night."

He grinned, a flash of white teeth against his

golden skin. "I'm glad you're so easily impressed. Come on, let's step up the pace, stretch our legs."

We swung along south, then cut west through the trees that marked the end of my property.

"Careful where you step," he admonished. "The closer we get to the ocean, the rockier it is."

"Are you sure my land goes this far?" I asked as we approached a building I hadn't seen before because it was shielded from the house by the trees.

"Positive. Remember, I play chess with your lawyer."

"And you pump him for free information over the chessboard?" I laughed.

"Well, it works both ways, you know," Philip said complainingly. "When we were finished with your boundaries I was obliged to listen to Elmer's troubles with his sinus cavities. I paid for his services, you can bet. Yes, my dear, that cottage is definitely yours."

I sprang away gleefully. "Then there's my sixth gate!"

Philip ran after me. "I thought you'd decided the place wouldn't have seven gates. But you're right. There is, or was, a gate. It seems to have fallen to bits."

The cottage wasn't much to look at—small, nearly square, and sadly in need of paint and repair.

"Philip, do you think there's anything in it?"

"You *are* excited. You're like a child on a treasure hunt," he said with a pseudo-bored tone, but I noticed he was first to try the door. "It's locked!"

"Well, of course it's locked." I laughed at his crestfallen attitude. "I suppose the key is in that infernal black pocket of Erna's. I wish she'd just give me the whole bunch of keys. She always seems to have just one more."

"Ask her for them." Philip was futilely trying to pry loose one of the boards over the window on the little porch.

"It's just like you to be so darned logical. Now why didn't I think of that?"

"Because you're afraid of her," he suggested gently.

Exasperated, I started to protest, but his observation was at least partly true. "I guess I do find her intimidating, but that's going to cease. The instant I get back to the house I'm going to demand that she turn over all the keys, not keep dredging them up one at a time and doling them out like candy to a child. It *is* my house!"

"'Atta girl. Up and at 'em!" He looked at his watch and grimaced.

"Is it late? I can gather up the blanket and things if you need to rush."

He kissed me. "You're a hundred percent, do you know that?"

"Well, I'd hate to think I was only fifty. Run along. I'll see you later."

I walked slowly back toward the cliff. It was going to be a foggy night; already the sun was disappearing in surging gray rolls of mist.

Seven Gates, I mused. Did the original owner of the house name it so in honor of the tentmaker? Or were there really *seven* gates on the property? I remembered another line from the *Rubaiyat*:

There was the Door to which I found no key;
There was the Veil through which I might not see:

There were many veils though which I could not see, too many. I would have given a greal deal for the key to open the door to the mystery of Joanna, her obsession of whatever sort it was, and to the goings-on in her former home. I had to keep my wits about me and lay aside the fears, conquer my inclination to let my imagination run wild.

There was a small library on the second floor of Seven Gates. I promised myself if I found a copy of the *Rubaiyat* I would forget about the seventh gate.

As I carried the blanket and the basket to the house, I thought back over my afternoon with Philip. I was no longer doubtful of my love for him; this time I wouldn't be disappointed. I recalled suddenly that he had never answered me about the key to Joanna's room. It didn't matter; I trusted him implicitly.

CHAPTER TEN

THE FOG pressed its wet gray silence against the house. I had changed from the cool sleeveless blouse I had worn on the picnic with Philip to a warm yellow sweater. Erna was on her knees in front of the fireplace in the brown parlor.

"There, that'll catch now. Nothing like a fire to keep away the chill from the fog. Chimney seems to draw all right." She stood up and turned to me. "Well, now, ain't that a cheery color! Does make your eyes yellow. Cat's eyes. Don't live up to them, though, you don't."

Offended, I flared, "What do you mean, I don't live up to my eyes?" Really, this woman was sometimes more than I could bear. Just as she would win me over, she would become insufferably rude.

"Hah, got your back up," she cackled. "And here I thought you had no spunk at all! Glad to see a little get up and go. You look like Joanna, but you're maybe more like your mother."

"Who had no spunk, I suppose," I snapped.

"Not much. She used to let Joanna use her something pitiful when they were kids. Of course, Leanna was sweet and gentle, but then she could use that sometimes. Still, I hate to see you let people take you over like you do."

I wanted to laugh. Who had taken me over, as she

put it, more than Erna herself! I was furious with her, yet my fury sputtered out against the facts. She was right. I nearly always let people have their way and if I did feel anger I seldom spoke up about it, though I had often burned for days inside, thinking of the devastating words that would have put the recipient of my anger in his place—had I ever uttered those words aloud.

"Well, girl, spit it out! You're mad, I can see that. Would be myself in your place." Her dark eyes glittered in their deep sockets as she baited me.

"Of course I'm angry," I said stiffly.

She sniffed. "Don't think you know how to be."

"I don't suppose it's necessary to screech and throw the crockery just because you sit there and criticize not only me but my mother."

Erna cocked her head to one side. "Not sure I was critical. I was very fond of Leanna; I just felt sorry for her sometimes."

"Well, neither of us needs your pity, particularly not my mother!" Scalding tears built up painfully. I grabbed the art paper I had brought and drew furious, if blurred, Christmas trees as I swallowed back my bitterness.

I started as I felt the pat on my shoulder. Erna didn't say anything, but when I looked up after a time she was sitting across the room, her skinny legs stretched out in front of her, working her thin lips in and out, obviously deep in thought. As if she felt my eyes on her, she looked up.

"I should think you'd need more light than the kerosene lamps, even the both of them, for drawing pictures."

I figured that interest in my work was as near to a

verbal apology as I was likely to get from her, so I decided to accept it. "I'm only sketching, but I'd never be able to do any color work at night. Which brings up the question of when they are going to fix the electrical lines. It seems to me they've had plenty of time."

"Does, at that. I'll check up on it."

"Or I can when I go into Silver City with Philip. By the way, Philip looked up some verses that made me think maybe Seven Gates was named for them rather than the actual number of gates on the grounds. I was going to see if the library had the book."

"Omar Khayyam," she said with a far-off look in her eyes.

Surprised, I asked, "You know it?"

"Of course I do!" she answered with some asperity. "I never imagined it to have anything to do with Seven Gates, though. Suppose it could, but I never got the notion the old captain was especially well-read or impressed with mysticism of that sort. But then, I never knew him: he was dead long before my time. Just heard the stories—bit of a tartar, I thought."

The yellow light wasn't the best for artistic endeavors, so I put my drawings aside. "I think I'll just go up to the library now and have a look. I didn't really notice what sort of books were there when we were looking for Joanna's portrait."

Erna got up and smoothed her black dress, which was fading to a charcoal gray across her bent shoulders. "I believe I'll just trot along. Might be I'll find something to read I haven't read since I was knee high to a grasshopper."

We each picked up a lamp. I gathered my drawing materials and prepared to take them upstairs.

"You aiming to stay upstairs?" Erna asked.

"I think so. Shall we lock up? The fire's about out, and unless you had something to do down here. . . ."

"No. Might as well lock up then. I'll get the back door."

I had found a hook just inside the front door and had hung my key there. As I twisted the lock I thought, *ask her for the rest of the keys.* I heard her banging around in the kitchen, the screen door resisting the final half inch as it always did, the inside door slamming, the rattle of a pot against the stove.

"Go on ahead. I'll just fix up the coffee for morning," she called.

Chagrined, I trooped up the steps. It was as if she'd read my mind, not for the first time. I would have to put off standing up for myself on the matter of the keys for the time being, but I would confront her about them when she joined me in the library.

The room was not large, and only one wall was shelved. I set the lamp, which gave off a smudge of smoke that blackened the glass chimney on one side, on a piecrust table between two wingback chairs. The illumination was barely adequate, and I found myself straining to see the titles of some of the older books whose gold lettering had tarnished with time. There seemed to be no particular order to the placing of the volumes, either by author or subject matter, something that I vowed to remedy within the next day or two. I started at the top row, squinting in the dim light, and was thoroughly engrossed when Erna came in.

"More light will help," she said, placing her lamp

on the leather-topped desk that dominated the west side of the room where the wall separated it from Joanna's bedroom.

I nodded and continued by browsing, pulling down a book now and again in a companionable silence that Erna finally dispelled.

"Don't see the book you're looking for. Don't remember that I ever saw it here, either, and I think I read most every one at one time or another."

"No, I haven't run across it. I don't believe it's here.I think in a way I'm glad. There is a certain excitement to searching out the seventh gate. No doubt a holdover from my childhood—making mysteries where none exist."

"Oh, I don't know. . . ."

Something bumped in the next room. I froze, my hand outstretched toward a book I had been about to choose to take to my room.

"What was that!" Erna's voice was sharp.

My heart was hammering in my ears so that I hardly heard my own shaky voice. "I . . . don't know. I don't hear anything now."

We both stood listening. Erna's face had lost color; it was apparent even in the yellow, inadequate light from the lamps. I longed to be able to walk to the switch on the wall by the door and flood the room with modern, shadow-clearing white light.

"Must have been a mouse," I ventured, saying the only thing that would come to words.

Erna shook her head. "Maybe it didn't come from in there," she said thinly. "Probably. . . ." She got no further.

It bumped again and I flew at her, scarcely breathing. There was a series of shuffling sounds that grew fainter and farther away, until there was an empty silence. The seconds dragged while Erna's scrawny arms tightened around me, and she patted with an automatic rhythm. It was I who eventually pulled away.

"I. . . ." I swallowed and tried again. "Shouldn't we. . .?"

"You *did* lock the front door?" she quaked, but with a real attempt at firmness.

I nodded as I picked up one of the lamps with two shaking hands. "It—it sounded like. . .like they—he went downstairs."

Erna was looking around, then went to the small fireplace and picked up the poker that leaned against the red brick. She went to the door and opened it slowly while I held out the light to illuminate as much of the hall as possible. There was no one there.

The long hall stretched darkly, the faint ghostly shapes of occasional tables and little chairs bumped out from the walls.

"We have to look in there," I whispered with a nod toward Joanna's room.

Poker raised, the lamp casting eerie shadows before her, Erna took short wary steps in the direction of Joanna's room.

"The key! I don't have it." Even though I kept my voice low, it sounded loud in the dark silence of the old house.

I heard a clinking sound, then Erna held up a bunch of keys for me to see. We were outside the door, listening, hearing nothing but the usual creakings and groanings I had come to accept as part of Seven Gates. After a long hesitation she inserted the key. The lock resisted long enough to get my hopes up that we might be unable to enter, then it gave way to her metallic twistings and the door squeaked open, a noise that sent my heart to my throat once again.

"Damn the light!" I held the lamp at arm's length into the room. It left the corners shadowy dark. "I don't see anyone here."

"Don't see any portrait, either," said Erna in an almost normal tone.

I felt as if I'd swallowed an ice cube and my hand shook, sloshing the kerosene in the lamp.

"Here, don't drop that lamp! You'll have us afire. Get hold of yourself, girl."

"Who's doing this to me?" I croaked fearfully.

"Here, give me that lamp." Erna took it from me, and holding her poker aloft she went to the center of the room, then moved slowly toward the bed.

"My God!"

Erna stood stock-still, then with a clatter set down the lamp on the long blond dresser. Her mouth was a thin line of terror as she advanced upon the motionless mound under the covers. She poked at the lump, then grabbed the rumpled bedspread and jerked it off the still form.

I cowered in the doorway, my heart nearly stopped, overcome with horror, my hands stifling my hoarse cry.

"Pillows!" she announced disgustedly, then picked up something and held it to the light. She slowly put her hand through the crown of a dark hat, through a long rent in a widebrimmed woman's hat.

I found my voice. "It's Joanna's, isn't it?"

"Maybe, maybe not." She threw it back on the bed, retrieved the poker she had put aside when she picked up the hat, and scooped up the smoking lamp.

"We'd best pull ourselves together and go through the house." She stopped, then bent down, squinting in the dim light. She gave something a little kick and it skittered toward me, stopping near my feet.

I bent my quaking knees and plucked the object from the floor. "A jackknife! Whose is it?" I asked inanely.

"Well, if we knew that, we'd know a whole lot, wouldn't we?"

Again she suggested we pull ourselves together to search the house. I assumed she meant *I* should pull myself together, as she appeared to be quite in command of herself, so I made an effort to stop my shaking and said I'd get the second lamp from the library.

"I'll come along," she offered. "Then we better refill the both of them. We'll start downstairs and make sure they're gone. I think you were right. It did sound like somebody went down the steps."

When we were refilling the lamps in the kitchen Erna said suddenly, "You should get out of this house!"

I heard myself saying, "No! I can't go!" when I wanted more than anything to be away from the lurking terror I had felt at every corner, at every doorway as we had made our way downstairs from that awful upper room.

"Why not? You're scared to death!"

"I know, but I can't leave."

And it was true, I couldn't go. As we shone our pitiful lights into room after room I tried to reason with myself. It made sense to go away. There was a definite threat hanging over me; why else the hatchet buried in the table, why else the gash in that hat? Was someone trying to frighten me away for some reason? Or was it something quite different?

As we went through Seven Gates, through the rooms where Joanna had lived, and one in which she had died so violently, I could feel her presence as if she walked in my shadow, just out of the revelation of the lamps.

The house was empty and we finally parted, Erna and I, and entered our bedrooms. Whether she slept or not, I don't know. I did not. Toward dawn I was so distraught I promised Joanna I would avenge her death. I was convinced it had been she who had perpetrated the happenings, much as she had played the pranks on her sister when they were children.

"I will avenge your death, Joanna, if that's what you want. If I haven't interpreted what you're trying to tell me, then give me another sign."

IN THE LIGHT OF MORNING, my promise and wild imaginings seemed a little absurd. Joanna wouldn't have dropped a jackknife.

It lay in my hand, small, with a black plastic handle.

"Is this yours, Elijah?"

"Nope." He dug in his pocket and came up with a knife of some size with a bone-colored grip. "Looks like some kid's."

"Ollie's or Mark's, do you think?"

"Couldn't say. Might be."

"Well, would you ask them to come and see me if you see them?"

"Make a point of it if you want."

We agreed on that and he left. I glanced at Erna, who was rolling pie dough on the linoleum kitchen counter.

"It's possible," she said. "They have the reputation of being scamps."

"I sincerely hope it's that simple. Was it Joanna's hat?"

"It was. I threw it out this morning after I looked at it in good light. Got it a couple years before. . . she died. Don't remember she'd worn it after the first few months. The styles changed. Somebody must have taken it from a bundle given to charity or something. Beats me. Still think I'd leave if I were you."

"Well, you're not me."

She shrugged. "No, I'm not."

"You don't have to stay, you know," I said, and held my breath for fear she would take me at my word.

She waved her floury hand as if to say there was no question about her staying.

"Well, you wanted me to be more like Joanna, have more spunk, you said."

"I take it back."

"It's too late."

Her head came up and her fanatic eyes glimmered in the morning light from the east windows. "I hope not," she said in her deep Cassandra-like voice. "I hope not."

I shuddered a little at the implication in her somber tone. Then I asked, "How did you get the key to Joanna's room? I thought I had. . . lost it."

"I didn't get it back. I remembered that the key to my old room used to fit both doors if you jiggled it long enough."

"Oh." I couldn't stop my widened eyes from glancing at her. Her agate stare caught and challenged me.

I turned away. I was being stupid. Erna had been with me; she couldn't have anything to do with the horrors going on in this house. My mind was becoming too confused to think straight.

CHAPTER ELEVEN

THE NEXT AFTERNOON I stared unfocused into the kitchen cupboard. All these things Joanna had used before me; Joanna, whose flesh was shaped like my flesh, who had felt the same longings. I saw from eyes like hers the cups and plates she had seen. It would not be illogical to think I might have been created to take her place, to finish the life she had begun, created from her spirit. Reincarnation, perhaps, as Mark's mother had said. It was not unfeasible.

I started as a knock at the screen door interrupted my musings.

"Come in, boys. Would you like some cake? I just made it. I'm glad you got my message."

Mark looked at me suspiciously. "Ma told us Elijah said we better get on over here or else."

"That's not quite the way I worded the invitation, but I see it got results."

I studied the boys' faces covertly as I made a business of testing the knife by sectioning the cake. Neither displayed any particular uneasiness or guilt. I had intended to confront them right out, demanding to know if they had been behind the horrible incident of the night before. Between the two of them they could carry the painting around, but it would be an awkward procedure. But why? A game? It had all gone rather far for childish pranks, I thought. Then who? It seemed more likely, in the daylight, that it was someone this side of the mystical seventh gate. It was difficult to conjure up spirits in the sunlight, even as spunky a spirit as Joanna's would have to be.

I mentally ran down the list. Elijah? How would he gain if he frightened me away? Erna. There was her possessiveness about the house, and there was some element in her relationship with Joanna and myself that I hadn't been able to fathom. Opportunity? Only part of the time, but could she be working with another? It didn't make much sense. Jeffery had threatened me, but he was far away, and the objects that were used to set up the terrorizing scenes were all tied up with Joanna. To my knowledge he knew nothing at all about my aunt. Joanna? I refused to even think about it.

"Shall we take the cake into the dining room? Here, bring the plates, and, Ollie, why don't you get forks out of that drawer there. Good." I had taken in the coffee pot for me and a pitcher of milk for the boys. I got down glasses and a thin china cup and saucer from the tall Queen Anne china cabinet. "Now, I asked you to come over because I wanted to talk to you."

Ollie attacked his cake, the first bite liberally decorating his dark angel's face with devil's food crumbs and moist fudge frosting. He looked to Mark to speak.

"What about?" Even Mark appeared more interested in the treat than the talk.

I had the jackknife in my pocket. I turned my palm over and held it out. "Any idea who this belongs to?"

"Hey, that's mine!" cried Ollie, spraying crumbs on the table and down his T-shirt.

A cold lick of disappointment dabbed at me. I hadn't wanted it to be them. I realized that I genuinely liked them, even admired their brave play. "Are you sure it's yours? Absolutely sure?"

" 'Course he's sure. He's been looking for it for a week," Mark assured me scornfully.

"Oh," I said with relief, "he lost it!"

"Ain't no other reason to be hunting for it," Mark said with finality. "Is that all you wanted us for? To give Ollie back his knife?"

"Not quite." The conversation was sprinkling the table with crumbs. With what I considered to be a great deal of tact, I suggested, "Since it's not polite to talk with our mouths full, suppose I tell you when we're finished with our cake."

Both boys nodded and bent to their work.

When Ollie, who had had a head start and had let his partner do most of the talking, pushed his plate back, he asked with wide, innocent brown eyes, "Where did you find my knife?"

Mark looked up and reached for his milk. "Yeah, where?"

The boys were seated across from me and I could watch the expressions of both. "In the room where my aunt was killed."

Surprise opened a pair of sea-colored eyes and a pair of dark ones.

"Couldn't have! We haven't been in there since.... When did you find it?" Mark demanded with a blustery show of bravado intended, I was sure, to muddle me so I wouldn't remember the admission that they had ever been in that room.

"Last night."

"We was home last night."

"And we can prove it," injected Ollie hopefully.

"But you are dead certain that it's yours?"

So far neither child had picked up the knife. It lay in the middle of the table. Ollie's slender, olive-toned hand reached out, then drew back.

"The littlest blade is broke off," he said.

Mark took the knife and drew a blade from the black plastic handle. It was intact. Then, while I winced, he used a fork to pry out a stub of a blade.

"See?" they spoke in unison.

"I see. And how long ago were you in my house, in Joanna's room?"

Both boys became very occupied with picking up crumbs from the table and carefully placing them on their plates.

"Last summer," Mark mumbled.

"Before we saw the ghost. We were too scared. . . ."

Mark shut him off with a sharp gesture. "What's this third degree all about, anyway? And just remember, we got an alibi for all last night!"

I wanted to laugh, but I knew if I gave in to it I would lose the boys forever. I wondered if Mark realized he was giving a most credible imitation of Humphrey Bogart. I doubted it; they were too young. Their impressions of tough guys would come from television heroes.

"I'm glad you do have alibis," I said. "You may need them, because something quite serious happened here last night." I decided to leave out the pillow dummy on the bed and the murdered hat, for murdered was the way I thought about it. I told them only that the portrait had been stolen.

"That great big picture? Who would want it?"

Ollie spoke up. "I would. She's awful pretty and...." He withered under a burning look from his leader.

But Ollie's admission convinced me of their innocence, at least in regard to last night's escapade, although I wouldn't put much past them.

"Do you want us to help you look for the picture?" asked Mark, once he'd shushed his friend.

"We've searched the house, I'm afraid. It's not something you can hide in a drawer. It's pretty big." I thought of the boarded cottage. I didn't think we would find Joanna there, but I did have something to make up to them, I felt, for having suspected them of what was obviously not their crime. "Tell you what; you know that cottage down past the trees?"

"The first-mate's house."

"That's the one. If you two want to help get a board or two off the window, we could look in there."

"Couldn't you just unlock it? It belongs to you, doesn't it?"

I suddenly remembered I had been about to ask Erna for my keys last night when that awful incident had occurred. I *wouldn't* admit I hadn't possession of my own keys!

"I don't have the key to that house. I believe it has been lost."

Mark hitched up cutoff jeans. "I think we ought to see the scene of the crime."

Dubious, I hesitated. "The door's locked and...I gave the key to someone and he forgot...."

"When?" The sea-colored eyes glinted as he pounced on the last word.

"A few days ago, but...."

"Who?"

Wearily, I admitted, "Dr. McCarney."

"Oh." He was clearly let down. "No, it ain't Doc."

I laughed a little shrilly. "I'm relieved to hear you say that. Not that I ever believed it was."

"Well, I should hope not. Doc wouldn't want to scare you. He's *besotted* with you."

"Besotted!"

"Ma said so." Ma seemed to carry a lot of weight, as both boys nodded gravely in time with each other. "Anyway, it don't matter about the key." The towhead dived a grimy hand into his pocket. "This one fits pretty good," he said, choosing one key from an assortment.

My mouth fell open with dismay.

"Now, don't you go thinking things! Ma knows I was home last night. She had me shelling nuts for a bunch of cakes she had to make for that dumb society she belongs to."

This time I did laugh. "Now, that's an alibi! No, I won't go thinking things. Shall we ascend to the scene of the crime, then?"

They raised two pairs of young brows, bleached white and dark silky brown.

"Go upstairs," I explained.

Mark was right. The key fit with a little jiggling. He went inside Joanna's room without hesitation; Ollie followed one wary step at a time. I stayed in the doorway, holding my breath, half expecting the capricious portrait to have returned to its place above the mantle.

"Well, she's been stole, all right," Mark pronounced.

"Is it worth a lot of money?" asked Ollie.

"I shouldn't think so. I think it's been moved for a different kind of reason. It's not the first time it's disappeared," I admitted, deciding that they deserved a little more truth than they were getting. I told them about my encounter with Joanna at the head of the stairs, her subsequent disappearance, and return to her own room.

"Somebody's trying to scare you, or it's worth more money than you think, or maybe somebody just wanted it." We had started toward the staircase. Mark stopped and eyed the wall at the landing. "I don't see where it could have hung."

"I forgot to mention there was no evidence that I wasn't seeing things," I said acidly.

Mark measured me with his eyes. "I never said you didn't see it there; I said I couldn't see where it was hung from."

"You have a very logical approach to things, I see. Well, I hope you figure out which of the three motives is the real one, and how the portrait was there on that wall when it couldn't possibly have been."

"The ghost. . . ."

"Now, that's *not* logical. You disappoint me, Holmes," I said, chattering brightly. "Anyone for more cake before we go down to the cottage?"

AFTER THE SECOND ROUND of chocolate cake we found some tools and walked toward the trees that hid the first-mate's house from Seven Gates. When we reached it the boys fell to work with gusto, prying nails out of the old boards as high as they could reach. I took my turn with the top of the boards and we removed the covering to find a dirt-streaked, locked window.

"Now what!" I demanded in frustration.

I didn't get any answer from Ollie. In his excitement he was dancing from one foot to the other and rubbing his hands together with undisguised glee. Mark's answer was action. He calmly placed a nail puller between the window sash and the peeling frame. By jimmying it patiently, he soon had the window up with remarkably little evidence of forced entry. I trembled mentally at what this boy could become, and I made up my mind to stop encouraging these adventures. What a little pirate he was!

"You want to go in first?" he asked politely.

"Go ahead, both of you."

Mark disappeared into the gloomy interior, Ollie at his heels. I carefully swung one leg over the sill. The boys stood in the middle of the room, hushed, as if they expected to come upon the bones of the old first mate—or at the very least, his ghost or his treasure. I peered through the dimness thinking, *John Wilde would have a field day here. If ever I needed to raise money. . . .*

Mark was advancing toward a dusty blackened fireplace.

"Don't touch that!" I yelled.

His hand stopped in midair, six inches from the hatchet. It lay on the brick hearth as if thrown there carelessly. The rest of the room was neat, though covered with a thick layer of dust.

Mark stayed in his tracks, squinting. "Don't anybody move!"

I moved. I brought my other leg over the sill and into the room, and watched the boy.

"Maybe there's fingerprints," whispered Ollie, frozen where he stood.

"I'm looking for footprints," said Mark, his soprano deepened with importance. "And I found some."

He was right. Someone had been walking around, disturbing the dust of years, quite recently.

"Who's got a key to this place?" he demanded.

"Well, Erna, I suppose." I was content to have him do the detecting. All I felt like doing was running all the way back to Chicago.

"She got big feet?"

I shrugged. "I don't know. She's tall; she wouldn't be wearing a size five. I suppose she has good-sized feet."

"Hmm. I'm going to have a look around for that picture. Don't nobody step on those tracks." He disappeared into the next room, whipping out a pen-sized flashlight with all the appearance of drawing a six-shooter.

Ollie and I looked impotently at each other, each waiting for the other to make the first move to get out into the sunshine. We stayed put. After an eternity Mark was back, his towhead the only bright thing in that ill-lit room.

"Nope, didn't see no picture. Leastways not that one." Apparently undaunted by the discovery of the hatchet, he went on, "The old man who lived here, he didn't die till he was a hundred. He was here when *she* got killed. He knew who did it. My grandma said so, said he told her he did. He knew, but he wouldn't tell."

"That seems to make two people who wouldn't tell, though Erna claims her man didn't do it. Odd. But tell me, not about the murder, Erna told me about that. What about the person you saw that night on the widow's walk?"

"You mean the ghost?"

Grudgingly I said, "If you must have it that she was a ghost. What was she wearing, for instance?"

"Smoke," said Ollie.

"'Twas not! A sort of yellowish dress and it blew around."

"Yellowish?"

"Yeah, the same color you wear a lot. The same dress she was wearing in the picture, maybe. Or like it, anyway. Yellowish."

"Amber?"

"I guess that's what you call it."

I swallowed around a lump of dread and asked, "Did you see her face?"

The boy screwed up his face in thought. "Uh-uh. She had real long hair, black like yours, and it was blowing around. Didn't see no face at all."

"It couldn't have been Erna inspecting the house?"

He threw me a withering glance. "At midnight? Anyway, the ghost was. . . ." At a loss for words this grimy, raggedy urchin fluttered and balleted with touching natural grace.

"Graceful and beautiful," I provided.

"Yeah."

"You certainly saw a lot for the middle of the night, especially when I understood that you 'lit out.' . . ."

"I always see a lot. I *observe*," he said without a hint of self-importance.

Ollie had one leg over the windowsill. I longed to follow suit, but I wouldn't give ground until Mark moved up behind his friend and nudged him into completing his exit. Then he stood back while I scrambled over the sill. Mark brought up the rear and closed the window.

"You boys can hang on to the tools if you want, and work on unboarding the rest of the windows when you feel like it."

Mark let out a war whoop.

"But please don't go inside unless I'm with you! Promise?"

"Okay." Two heads nodded without enthusiasm.

"Then for your trouble you can pick out something in there to keep."

"Oh, boy! Can I have the compass?" shouted Mark.

More quietly, Ollie asked for the fishing rod that stood in a corner.

We parted at the side of the cottage, the boys heading for home down the beach, while I walked slowly back to the main house. I wondered if I should call the local police and tell them about the episodes with the hatchet and its whereabouts, but the murder had been so long ago. That ax could hardly be the murder weapon itself. Surely they had found it and would scarcely put it back into circulation. I thought that one just never wondered about what actually happens to the butcher knives, the bookends, the everyday items people use to kill each other. It gave me a chill to think about it.

There had to be copies of the newspapers that carried the story twenty-six years ago. *I am going to make a point of looking them up*, I thought as I walked slowly back to Seven Gates, where nothing ever seemed to stay safely in the past.

The footprints in the dust seemed to reveal nothing more than the fact that someone had been in the house, someone whose feet were not small. That could be more than half the adults in the country. The locked door pointed toward Erna; she had the key. But the boys had proved to me that these old-fashioned locks posed few problems to an enterprising person with a handful of rusty old keys.

As I walked through the trees, the sun was moving toward the horizon, taking its golden warmth with it and leaving a thin chill in the air. This was a place of contrast, warm sun and chilly ocean breezes, a place where a sweater could be suddenly welcome, but I hadn't learned to prepare for that yet. I hugged my arms to my body and picked up my pace. I envied Joanna wherever she was hidden, safe in her gilt frame, neither cold nor hot nor frightened; just smiling.

THE NEXT MORNING, just before lunch, I administered the final brush stroke. Erna's portrait was as yet unframed. I turned it to get the best light from the French window, my stomach tightening. It was the first serious painting I had attempted for several years, and I was afraid to look at it closely for fear of being disappointed. I had thought I had accepted being a good commercial artist when my dream was to be a fine painter. I kept my eyes averted as I turned the easel, but finally I had to step back and really look.

Cassandra in the sun leaped into my vision and tore at my emotions.

Dry sobs escaped my throat. "Oh, it's good! It's really good!" I clenched my fists at my sides. I had to get control of myself. It was the height of silliness to sob when I should be laughing for joy. "Erna!" I started to run down the stairs, then slowed to a more sedate walk.

"My word, girl, no need to shout! What do you want?"

Had she thrown cold water over me it would have had the same effect. I stood very straight; even my voice sounded straight to me as I said coolly, "Have you seen your portrait yet?"

"No. Artists don't like to show a work until it's done. Figured you'd tell me when it was ready to look at."

"It's ready. Do you want to see it?"

"Well, it's mine, ain't it?" She removed her apron and stuck her wild hairpins more tightly into her bun. She even smoothed her faded black dress over her hips before she started up the stairs.

My feet suddenly froze halfway up. What if she

didn't like it? She wouldn't see herself in the mirror the way I saw her when her fervency lighted up her cavernous face. She wouldn't see the zealot's eyes; she would see only an old woman, leathered and homely. Had I really seen anything different? I had been wrong; the painting was no good. I should have known better than to try anything more than simple card scenes. I was an adequate craftsman, nothing more.

I was still rooted to the step when Erna came out of the telescope room and started slowly down the steps toward me. She didn't say a word. Her birdlike eyes might as well have been blind for all they saw of me. She passed me, brushing against my arm, and I could hear that she went through the house and out the front door.

I clung to the banister, trembling. "I've made her angry. Whatever possessed me to paint that thing! Heaven knows what she'll do now."

I cursed the day I had asked her to stay with me. Better if I had fallen, or thrown myself over the useless railing onto the widow's walk.

My arm jerked violently and I started. It was as if a strong hand had grabbed me and given me a shake. There was no one there; I was alone on the gloomy stairs.

I told myself it was an involuntary movement caused by the state of my nerves. I said it to myself and aloud, but I didn't quite believe it. Just so would Joanna had shaken me out of my morbid thoughts had she been alive. It wasn't illogical that she, who was so strong in life, could have strength to reach through that seventh veil through which most of us could not see.

Erna returned a short while later, but I took to my bed for the rest of the day, pleading a headache that I then proceeded to get, and which I felt I richly deserved.

Erna administered the medication and homemade soup in a distracted manner. Neither of us mentioned the portrait.

CHAPTER TWELVE

I LAZILY watched the sun and shadow play hide-and-seek on the rocks in the grotto I had found among the trees bordering my property on the side next to the road. One rock was flat, a table, while others of smaller size lay scattered like Roman lounges. I heard footsteps crunching through the pine needes.

"Philip? You're late," I said, not bothering to look up.

Silence was my answer. Even the wind stopped to listen.

"Philip!"

I sprang up and stared in a circle around me. There was no one there, but there *was* something lying on the ground near the edge of the grotto—dropped, I decided, by the passerby who had gone on, perhaps smiling at my mistaken call. I hurried to pick up the bundle and call after whoever had dropped it. I shook it out into billows of amber chiffon.

"A dress!"

The footsteps had sounded heavy and masculine, but that might have been because I had been expecting them to be Philip's. I looked around once more for the owner, but I realized that my calling out had disguised the direction of his retreat. I held out the garment so I could see it better. The recurrent breeze stirred and fluttered the filmy material. It was an evening dress, though shorter than the ones I owned. It was cut round and low with flowing sleeves gathered at the wrists, and was caught at the waist with a beaded belt. The beads were bronze, a little dulled by time. It was of a style that was making a comeback after twenty years or so, but with those designer touches that precluded trotting out the contents of the attics and calling it fashion.

I held it up to me. It would fit perfectly.

Philip's voice startled me. "I thought we were going to the city to check on your lack of electricity, not to a dance. Though why we couldn't do both, I can't think. There is a dance on tonight at the local club."

Pressing the dress against me, I twirled. "It's lovely, isn't it? Someone dropped it, but I wasn't quick enough to call her back."

"Shall we wait awhile, then? She'll no doubt come dashing back when she realizes she's dropped it. But seriously, we do have something to celebrate. I had a patient! That's why I'm late."

He eyed one of the chair rocks, then opted for the pine needles and sat down. He held out his arms.

"Philip! That's marvelous!" I settled myself beside him. "We could wait a bit. I imagine the electric company is open until five."

"And I got an appointment for you with Dr. Smithers. I took another look at the X rays of your beautiful head and I could see nothing unusual. Still... that's not my field."

I was suddenly afraid. "You mean... the headaches.... You suspect a...?"

"Brain tumor?" he finished for me. "No, I do not. What I suspect is that you've been through a rough time, rougher on you than you'll admit, and it is taking its toll. Lea, I watched you in the garden that day. It frightened me. Your voice was...not your own." He laughed uneasily. "You really get into your parts. I didn't much care for Joanna—that is, your interpretation of the child. See, my darling, you've got me doing it, thinking of Joanna as alive, real. You're too good an actress. I think you've missed your calling."

I picked up a brittle pine needle and broke it into bits. "You sound like mother," I told him, then switched the subject. "We found the hatchet—*a* hatchet, anyway—the boys and I. It's in the cottage."

"Elijah probably put it there after he took it out of your table. It had to be put somewhere."

"I suppose so," I said absently. I hadn't told him about the fright Erna and I had had a few nights before, and I was reluctant to now. He would insist that I leave the area and I didn't want to argue about it. "That would mean he had a key to get in, and if he had that one, he might have keys to the whole house."

"One doesn't necessarily follow the other. I think he and the man who lived in the cottage were friends. I've heard Elijah speak of him, never by name. He seemed to have been known simply as the first mate."

I had assumed that the rent in the hat had been made with a hatchet, but any knife could have had the same effect. I couldn't see a grown man as down-to-earth as Elijah making pillow dummies and murdering them. It was a childish thing to do. None of it made sense.

"Do you think we might have time to look up the news stories on Joanna's murder while we're in town?"

He looked at me with narrowed eyes. "I guess so," he said reluctantly.

"It's not just morbid curiosity. I want to know, well, to find out what sort of details were made public."

"I can tell you that it was a big story. Anybody could conceivably have read it and set out to make you, shall we say, uncomfortable in the house. The why escapes me. That's where I bog down."

"Then you've seen the papers?"

"Yesterday. Erna told me about the noise and the pillows and the hat. I've been waiting for you to tell me. I began to think you weren't intending to."

He was gazing off into the trees, avoiding my eyes. I turned his head toward me. "Only because I was afraid you'd try to make me go back to Chicago, and I don't want to leave here."

"Just here?"

"There might be one more reason," I teased.

"Well, if it's six foot three and has an M.D. after its name, I'm satisfied." His kiss took my answer.

It was a little while later when he said, "I think we'd better get started. It doesn't look like the owner of the dress is coming back for it. You could put an ad in the weekly paper. But now, on to Silver City."

He helped me up and brushed the pine needles from his trousers, and we walked to the house arm in arm, where I quickly packed a case so I could change for the dance that evening.

I LEANED AGAINST the counter at the electric company, weakened with fury. "What do you mean, nobody told you to turn it on!"

"We have no order, ma'am, and no deposit," the lace-collared clerk said primly.

"Well, you have an order now!" I shouted.

"The deposit is twenty-five dollars," she insisted.

With trembling hands I took out my checkbook and dashed off a check, which the woman picked up carefully between her thumb and forefinger.

"This is an out-of-state check."

I let her get no further. "I want to see your supervisor—immediately!"

My voice, never as light and feminine as I desired, must have boomed over the pale green partitions, for a white-haired man appeared and came toward me.

"What seems to be the trouble here?"

I opened my mouth to tell him, but he was looking at his employee for his information, which she gave him quite succinctly.

"Seven Gates?" he said with surprise. "Why nobody's lived there for years."

"Well, I do, and I want the lights on—today!"

"Impossible. You see, the lines were taken down in a storm."

"So I heard," I interrupted coldly. "I suggest you put them back up!"

I stormed out and strode down the block to where Philip waited in the station wagon.

"Can you believe that!" I raged as I slammed the door shut.

"I could if I knew what you were talking about," Philip said quietly.

"Erna lied to me! She never even put in the order to have the power turned on!"

"Oh, come. Why would she do that?"

"Yes, why would she? Maybe so she could cave my

head in by lamplight! Maybe so I'd have to ask her to move in! Oh, I don't know!''

''Couldn't it be just a simple mistake?''

''She didn't pay the deposit!''

''No, that would be up to Elmer. I'll look into it tomorrow. Now, calm down or Dr. Smithers will clap you in the hospital for high blood pressure. Utility companies have no doubt mislaid turn-on orders before, and probably will again.'' He put his arms around me and nibbled my ear. ''Come on, sweet, we'll get it straightened out with Erna and Elmer tomorrow. Now, let's get you to the doctor, then we'll go out on the town. You brought your party clothes, didn't you?''

''I put everything in my overnight case.''

I was beginning to calm down, and I recalled that I'd had a difficult time getting the telephone in my apartment installed due to a mix-up in addresses. ''You're probably right. I'm just getting too nervy.''

He started the car and pulled into traffic. ''I suggest we come in another day to visit the library. I don't want you getting upset again today. Okay?''

''Okay.'' I put my head back and tried to relax. In a few minutes we pulled up in front of a tall building that had the unmistakable look of a medical building, efficient and sterile. Philip jumped out and opened my door.

''Here you are. Shall I wait in the coffee shop across the street or do you want me to come in?''

''The coffee shop, I think.''

''Good girl,'' he grinned. ''I know the kinds of magazines he subscribes to. Deadly.''

I laughed as he with his newspaper and I with my

overnight case containing my evening clothes went our separate ways.

The examination was routine; then I sat across the big desk from the pleasant, balding doctor.

"You seem a healthy young lady. Blood pressure a little high for your age. Anything to cause that?"

Shamefacedly I told him about my incident at the power company.

He grinned, but said nothing beyond suggesting that the reading be retaken next week to make sure it was simply temper. He told me my X rays looked perfectly normal, then said, "Now tell me about these headaches."

I did, though I left out the irrelevant things that started them.

He made notes and dismissed me, saying, "Next time you get one, I want to see you immediately. And take no medication."

"I don't have a phone yet and I have no car," I explained, wondering how I was to stand the pain until I could get into Silver City.

"It's important not to mask the symptoms," he said as he left the room.

I went back to my cubicle where I had made arrangements with the nurse to change into my long dress. I opened my overnighter and stepped back gasping. "That's not the dress I brought!"

I lifted out the amber waltz-length dress I had found in the grotto. I distinctly remembered folding my long white jersey because it wouldn't wrinkle. I shook the amber chiffon in anger. How could this happen? Erna? No, I recalled she had been off all afternoon on business of her own. I must have packed it myself. I had been hurried and a little distracted, my head full of things I wanted to say to Elijah about the cottage, nervous at seeing a strange doctor, besides feeling a bit guilty about going behind Erna's back to check on her claim to have been to the electric company.

I glared at the dress. There was nothing for it except to put it on.

It fitted to perfection. As I looked in the mirror I thought this might be the dress in Joanna's portrait. With everything else that had happened lately it wouldn't surprise me, and I was too exasperated to feel much upset about it if it were true. It was a simple dress, difficult to remember when I had been so arrested by the face.

I had been wearing my hair loose, but now I caught it back with a rubber band, and with a few pins I whirled a loose chignon. I peered at myself in the glass. I looked quite like Joanna. Except for the smile. But now I was on my way to meet Philip, my love, and he would put the smile on my face.

He had his nose buried in the newspaper as I approached the booth in the coffee shop. He looked up as I set my case on the table. His hazel eyes widened.

"You look beautiful, but why are you wearing—"

I interrupted him, "Because I'm losing my mind, that's why. I packed the wrong gown. I'm supposed to be dazzling you in white. I hope I don't look too dated."

"No, it's very like the things I've noticed in the ads, most up-to-date."

"Well, nearly. Perhaps that's what people will think anyway."

Philip dug into his pocket, then picked up his

check. "This doesn't seem to be your day, does it? Well, never mind."

"Sometimes I think it's been a long time since it's been my day," I grumbled.

As I waited for him to pay the cashier a queer thought popped into my mind. If it wasn't my day, whose was it? Joanna's? Was I wearing her dress? Perhaps tonight I would dance for her. One last dance for Joanna.

Philip took my elbow, bringing me back to reality of the moment. "What did Smithers have to say?"

"Nothing much. Said if I got another headache not to take anything, but to come in aching. I tried to explain about my isolation out there, but he expects me to grin and bear it."

"Precisely why I sent you to him. I couldn't stand to see you suffer."

In the car he gathered me into his arms. "You're smiling, Lea."

"Of course I'm smiling. I have a lover."

"So you have. And don't you forget it. I don't know if I want to share you with all those handsome men who will be trying for your attentions tonight. If anyone tries to cut in, I swear I'll knock him down."

Laughing, I said, "You may pout if you like, but please remain civilized. Anyway, we shall be so obviously in love, no one will dare."

THE MUSICIANS had taken their places and were sending out tentative notes into the crowd. I was restive and excited as I craned to look around me. The light was dim and somewhat pinkish, and red velvet was everywhere. The dance floor was large, surrounded on three sides by tables, now mostly cleared of all except twinkling glasses, a few raised in celebration. Philip had left me for a moment. There were several empty tables and a waiter was showing a small party to one of them. My breath jumped in my breast.

"Judy Garnett!"

How silly to feel jealousy; I had had assurance enough of Philip's love for me. Yet she still stirred a deep resentment when I saw her slender body draped and discreetly displayed in white. Thank goodness I had packed the wrong dress, I thought. Hers was a good deal like the one I had left behind.

She was with an older man and woman. My heart plunged into icy depths. Philip would be obliged to ask her to dance, as she obviously had no date.

"Damn!"

"What's that! Still mad about the dress?"

"Oh, no, as a matter of fact, I'm rather glad I packed this one now."

"It's extremely becoming, I'll say that. Ah, at last they're tuned up. Dance? You will tell if that ankle kicks up?"

I nodded as we whirled into an old-fashioned waltz among the first couples on the dance floor. Then the musicians settled into a more sedate medley and Philip held me close, moving almost in place to the music. His lips brushed my temple.

We were totally involved with each other, dancing about every other dance in deference to my ankle which held up very well. It was nearly eleven when I went to powder my nose.

When I returned, Philip's chair was empty. I thought little of that until, watching the dancers, I saw him dancing with Judy, his head bent to her buttercup hair. She looked up and smiled and their lips met briefly. They gazed tenderly at each other. My insides knotted while I pasted a smile on my lips.

How could he! He had said he loved me, yet the instant he let go of me, he was wrapped around that bright squirrel of a nurse. He wasn't any different from the rest of them. I half rose to run away, then remembered I had no way home. I would have to sit here, dance, talk gaily the rest of the evening—or make a scene. But I wouldn't give him the satisfaction. What would Joanna have done? I had half promised her this last evening of dancing. Joanna wouldn't have stood for this; she would have....

John Wilde appeared, bowing slightly, holding out his hand. "Why are we wasting this lovely music?" His eyes swept boldly over me as I stood up.

"Why, I hardly know," I sang out gaily. I twirled in front of him. "Do you like my dress, John?"

"It's most becoming. You know, you remind me...."

"Of Joanna?"

"My dear, in that dress you *are* Joanna!"

I returned his bold stare. "You're right, John, I am Joanna. I have come back to haunt you."

Just for a moment his tan seemed to fade. "With your charms, I hope you mean."

"Oh, with at least my charms," I said, glad for once that I had a throaty voice. I sent a side-glance at Philip, who was still engrossed with Judy. "No, tonight I am not Lea; I am Joanna. You knew her well. Will I do?" I made my eyes cling to John's exotic gaze. My body warmed in response to his overwhelming sensuality.

"Indeed you will do, Joanna-for-tonight; you will do very nicely," he purred. He danced us toward the musicians, gave them a signal and they switched to a tango. I gave my body up to John's and to the pulsing music. My body molded to his, feeling the movement of every muscle, following his every command, lost. It wasn't until the music faded away that I realized we were the only couple on the dance floor. Hand in hand we bowed, then John led me out to a balcony overlooking the moon-silvered sea.

"You tango superbly," he murmured, his hot lips brushing my fingertips.

I started to say, *but I don't tango at all*, which was too foolish, for I just had. Instead I said, "Joanna always dances well, does she not?"

His black glittering eyes looked hungrily into mine. "Joanna did...*does* many things well. Many things." His mouth took mine, gently, expertly, then searchingly until I lost all track of time and space.

"Lea!"

I broke from John's embrace, my heart fluttering, startled. Then I laughed softly as I looked around the balcony. "I'm terribly sorry, young man. You must have the wrong balcony. John and I are quite alone—and would like to keep it that way. Joanna doesn't like being interrupted...at anything."

I could feel a tremor pass through John's body.

"Lea...."

"Yes, that seems to be the lady's name. Have you seen her, John?" I was laughing as I looked at the bronze young man. "She may have come out here, but we really haven't seen her. We've been...occupied."

The very handsome young man turned on his heel and left.

John was staring at me. "You...you really *are* like...."

"Like whom, darling? I think I am like no one else. I am Joanna Brandt." I touched his chin playfully. "And you, of all people, must know there is no one like me in the entire world. No one. Shall we dance again?"

John held out his hand. He was obviously at a loss for words, but then I had always had that effect on him. I was the only woman who ever left John Wilde short of something to say.

I shook my hair free of the chignon as we left the balcony. "Do you like my hair this way, John? Just a bit shorter? It did give me such a headache, and Erna is so rough with the brush."

"Stunning," he said in a distracted way.

I frowned. I couldn't have him distracted. As we slipped into a slow dance I used my body to make sure of his full attention, and I got it.

I saw the bronze young man leaving the club. He was at least as good-looking as John, and he had a certain sensitivity about him that was appealing, but dangerous. Better that I stick to men like John. We were two of a kind. I noticed that Lea hadn't been found. Perhaps she, too, had wanted a stronger man. I had a moment's sorrow for the suffering young man, but I put it out of my mind when John swept me into another sensuous tango.

The music ended and the musicians left their places for a break.

John said, "I must be getting back to my table."

"Your table? You don't mean you're abandoning me?" I let my eyes linger on his lips.

"But your young man. . . ."

"My dear John, I thought *you* were my young man." My words were like thick honey, then I sharpened them into a stab I knew would hit the target. "However, if you prefer not to see me again. . . ."

"Ah, of course I prefer no such thing. I remember that temper, my little vixen."

I laughed, low and sensuously. "I am not little, but I will grant you the last."

"And I wouldn't have it any other way," he said as he relaxed and joined my laughter. "I'll find us a table alone, or we might go for a drive. You haven't seen my new car."

"No, I haven't. We'll take the drive. And John, *must* you make your apologies to that mouse of a woman I see staring at us?"

"Indeed not! In the radiance of your beauty I am blinded to little brown mice."

"Then let's run!" I grabbed his hand and we did run through the crowded club, causing much to-do and a calamity with a tray of drinks.

"Such fun! Did you see the look on that waiter's face!"

"I did. You are right. There is and there never will be anyone like you. Welcome home, Joanna. I don't know how you got here, but life has been scarcely worth living since your departure."

"My departure! You talk such nonsense, John!"

The parking valet brought around a low silver bullet of a car. My hair blew wild and free as John whipped the vehicle out of the parking lot and onto the open highway. We turned into the winding road above the ocean and plunged around the narrow turns, horn blaring, daring someone coming from the other direction.

"I do adore this car! Much nicer than your old one. What was it, John, I forget?"

"A. . . Packard?" he said as if he were not quite sure.

"How lovely to be so rich you have trouble remembering which car you drove last! In fact, how lovely it is that you're rich at all. You do know that is one of the things I like best about you, darling."

"I've always been aware of that, my dear. But sometime that sort of honesty is going to get your pretty neck. . . ."

I thought for a moment that his face whitened, but at that moment the moon pulled out of a cloud and washed silver over everything. John's hair in that light seemed more silver than I remembered. It had turned fast once it had started, but it was immeasurably more attractive that way.

"Well, I still must be honest, darling, even if it does upset people sometimes."

He pulled me against him and I leaned to touch my cheek to his. His hand caressed my bare shoulder as he nudged the chiffon down my arm, his fingers slipping, inching downward toward my breast.

I sat up. "Take me home!"

"Home!"

"Seven Gates. You remember. My hair is all tangled in the wind and I want Erna to brush it."

He laughed ruefully. "Someday, my darling. Some night."

"Well, not this night," I sparred. "Besides, if I gave in to you, it would be all over, wouldn't it? Don't think I don't know you, John Wilde. You pursue only as long as the prey runs."

Angrily, he spun the car around. "Not you. You have me half-domesticated already, you vixen."

"Now, John, one doesn't domesticate a leopard. One simply doesn't!"

He was silent for a time, then said, his voice carefully controlled, "In this case I am not sure who is the stalker and who is the prey, darling. You and I are just alike. One day you'll stop fighting me and then. . . ."

I laughed into the wind. "Yes, and then? Who knows?"

He pulled up near the gate to the back garden. Even in the moonlight I could see how unkempt it had become.

"I must get at Edward about the garden! How can it be I've let this go?"

John cleared his throat. "Lea. . . ."

"John, please! I know you aren't the faithful type, but you might at least remember my name!" I slammed the door of the luxurious car, and without waiting to be seen to the door, I stamped away.

He called after me in a wondering voice. "Edward hasn't worked here for over . . . for a very long time."

"Then I shall have to replace him quickly, won't I?"

I went around to the front door as I always did, for it didn't do to use the back, though Leanna would insist it didn't matter. And Erna used whichever door suited her at the moment. I had completely spoiled her for a servant, and I wondered sometimes if I shouldn't replace her. As long as I must go to an agency about getting another gardener, I might as well look into finding a more suitable lady's maid. Erna was such a chore at times. Still, she was fiercely loyal.

"Erna!" I called. "Come brush my hair. It got all tangled in the wind."

She appeared, blinking the sleep from her squinted eyes. She was holding a kerosene lamp.

"What, are the lights out again! Well, never mind. Come along to my room."

Erna looked positively dreadful, as if she'd aged twenty years. I did hope she wasn't going to get ill. Really, I should replace her.

She followed me up the stairs past the telescope room to my own.

"For heaven's sake, don't drop the lamp. Whatever is the matter with you? Give me that before you set the house on fire. You'd better go back to bed. I'll brush my own hair. It's easier now that I've cut it. It doesn't give me such fearful headaches."

She stood staring, her mouth open. "What are you doing in that dress?" she finally demanded.

"Wearing it, of course. What *is* wrong with you tonight? You look beastly. Better take something. I can't have you sick."

She drew away toward her own room down the hall.

I started to open the door of my room. "Erna! Someone's locked my door. Where's the key, for heaven's sake!"

"Hall table," her voice croaked.

"She is catching a cold. I certainly hope she doesn't give it to me," I muttered as I found the key half-hidden beneath the crocheted doily on the table.

Erna was taking the light with her as she moved away with the lamp. She stopped at her door.

"Where. . . ? Doc Philip. . ." she stuttered.

"What? Philip? Don't go away with that lamp until I get my door open. Philip? Do I know a Philip?" I supposed I must; I knew so many men. It made it all so confusing. Of course one had to pick one of them eventually. "Philip. Oh, yes, he's fine," I said to placate her, then I closed my door.

I opened the drapes and enough moonlight drifted in to see by. I found my silver brush on the vanity and brushed the tangles from my hair. It was more practical shorter; still, I felt an emptiness when the brush came too quickly to the ends. It had been so beautiful.

I took a white gown from the dresser drawer by feel and undressed, laying my party dress over a chair. As I pulled up the blankets I lay thinking.

John was a very exciting man, but I knew he would never do for a husband. More and more I wondered about the artist I had seen on the beach a few days ago. Would he really come to paint my portrait as he had promised? There was something different about Jay Savage, a quiet kind of strength. He wasn't like my wild friends, whom Leanna disliked for what she called their bad influence on me. It was easy for her to criticize now that she had a husband and no longer had to be in the swing of things.

I sighed. It would be so much easier if being a spinster were more acceptable. I should hate to have finally to take someone I didn't really love, just to be married. So many men to choose from, and I was bound to make a wrong choice.

And of course the artist didn't have a sou, I thought as sleep edged over into dreams.

CHAPTER THIRTEEN

THE SOUND of a door opening woke me. Late-morning sun slanted across a chartreuse bedspread.

"Oh, my God!"

Horror pinned me against the pillow. What was I doing in Joanna's room? What if the pain struck as it had before? But it hadn't. If I got out quickly....

"Uh, Lea?"

It was Erna with a breakfast tray.

I was prickly with the sweat of fear. "What am I doing in here?" The words came out hoarse and thick.

Erna spoke again from the doorway. "Do you want this in your own room, then?"

"Please." I got out of the dreadful bed and ran toward the telescope room. I dived under the familiar blankets and would have pulled them over my head if Erna hadn't been on my heels.

"I must have had too much to drink last night. Funny, all I remember is a little champagne."

Erna had the breakfast on a lap tray and she arranged it with a bit of a clatter over my legs. "That's all you remember?"

I put a hand to my forehead and tried to think. "I'm afraid so. Oh, Philip must be furious with me. I hope I didn't do anything awful. Oh, I wish we had a phone. I should call him and apologize. Or has he come?" I asked hopefully.

"No, he hasn't, but Elijah has. He's trimming the bushes out back," she said, her eyes on my every move.

I tried to stop my trembling. It had been such a fright to wake up in that room. But I had to pull myself together.

"I'm glad Elijah's here. I wanted to ask him about the key to the cottage, the first-mate's house. Do you have a key for it, by the way?"

"Nope. Oh, the phone's coming in Monday. Where do you want it? Used to be in the hall."

The fiasco at the electric company flooded back into my memory. I plucked up my courage to tell Erna I had checked up on her. "Ah, while I was in town, I stopped at the power company." I watched her eyes. Not a flicker.

"About time somebody checked up on them. Seems they're taking their sweet time."

I looked into my bowl of my spoon as I said, "They told me there had never been an order to turn it on. . . or a deposit made."

I jumped as she banged her fist on the night table beside me. "Idiots! I've a good mind to—"

"Who gave them the money?" I still stared carefully into the silver spoon.

"Why, Elmer, the lawyer. He wrote a check. We went special into town to take care of all that!"

I glanced up then. "You went together?"

She looked at me suspiciously. "We went together. I saw that prissy old maid take the check."

I smiled at Erna's calling anyone an old maid. "Well, now they have two. I wrote them another one."

"I'll see you get it back," she said stonily.

"Thank you, but I expect they'll find their error and return it." I figured while I was feeling relatively brave that it was a good time to ask her for all my keys. "I wonder if, since you're away sometimes, I shouldn't have all the keys to the place."

"No reason why not. Put them all on a big ring for you and got them all labeled. Don't know if we ever had one to the cottage. Long as I remember, it was rented out to that old man. Well over a hundred before he died, I understand." She dredged up a huge ring of carefully labeled keys and put them on the tray.

I was scarlet as I struggled to sound normal. "It doesn't matter about the cottage. Thank you. It must have taken you a long time to organize these keys and get them labeled like this."

She nodded vigorously, dropping a hairpin from her loose bun. "Took a deal of time just trying 'em out to see where they all went. But there they are!" Her eyes became small and squinty as she peered at me. "You feeling all right?"

I nodded. "Not even a hangover, which I richly deserve. Poor Philip! Oh, here's the key to Joanna's trunk!"

"Yes, but if I were you I'd leave it alone. And I expect you'll find me an interfering old woman, but I wouldn't sleep in there anymore. It's a pretty room. She'd just had it done over, but, well, it's better if you keep what's past in the past, if you know what I mean."

She looked at me sharply, as if I should know very well what she meant, but I thought I was missing something underneath the words she spoke.

"Mother used to say something like that. I really

don't know how I happened to go into that room after the dreadful experience of the other night. I don't even care for the decor, let alone its awful history. I like this room much better. I'll leave the champagne alone from now on. I just can't understand. . . ."

Erna patted my hand dryly. "You just rest. You've had a big grief, losing your mother."

Those ever lurking tears threatened again, but I flashed a bright smile. "Oh, I'm fine. Mother wouldn't want me to grieve."

She raised her sparse gray eyebrows. "Oh? Well, I don't reckon I'd have known her after all these years. Leanna. Such a pretty girl, so delicate, but I always thought she was pretty strong for all of that though. I don't know as she'd think it unseemly if you cried for her."

"Please," I said in a tight voice.

"Sure. You eat your oatmeal."

I swallowed my tears along with my cereal, all the time feeling Erna's birdlike eyes on me.

I TRIED TO REST, but physically I felt well and I grew nervous with inactivity. Finally I dressed in white slacks and a blouse that tied under the bust to show off the midriff. I tied my hair back with a yellow chiffon scarf and went downstairs. Erna shooed me out of the kitchen.

"You just rest; I think you overdid yesterday. I'm surprised at Philip. I'd have thought he'd be more careful of your health, him a doctor and all."

"Oh, I saw Dr. Smithers. He pretty well gave me a clean bill of health. And from now on I'll be extremely careful with the wine. Obviously it doesn't take much to. . . ." I trailed off as I went outside where I could hear Elijah snipping at the bushes in the garden.

"Morning," he said, straightening painfully, one horny hand at the small of his back.

"Good morning. You shouldn't work so hard around here."

"Wouldn't if I didn't want to. What are you up to today?"

Now that the time had come to ask him about the cottage key, I grew afraid. I had come to like Elijah tremendously. He just had to have a good explanation; it would be too much if I had to suspect him of deliberately terrorizing me. Nevertheless I had to ask him.

"As a matter of fact I was thinking about finishing up my explorations of the first-mate's cottage. But Erna doesn't have the key. We wondered if you might."

"Sure do." He patted various pockets in his denim overalls. "You want it?"

"It would make it easier to get in." I was smiling in relief. "The boys and I broke in."

"Noticed that. Wish you'd asked me for the key. Now I'll have to board it up again. Vandals, you know."

"I'm sorry. I didn't know you had it. The hatchet. . . ."

"Had to put it someplace. I didn't want you to see it again." He grinned fondly. "Didn't know you were going to vandalize the place."

"Well, it was thoughtful of you to get it out of sight. It did upset me to find it, I have to admit. Has Erna told you what happened the other night, the hat and. . . ?"

His eyes narrowed. "No. What did happen?"

I told him, finishing up, ". . . and I assumed it was the hatchet that was used to make the gash in the crown of the hat."

Elijah was silent for a moment, pushing his lips in and out in thought. "Where did you find the hatchet, exactly?"

"On the hearth."

"I left it in the bedroom closet."

My breath left me in a gasp. "Elijah! Who . . . ?"

"Don't know, but I sure mean to find out!" He looked at me speculatively. "You got any of your city friends down here?"

"No. That is, I hope not. My ex-fiancé did threaten me, after a fashion, but he wouldn't. . . ."

"Your ex-fiancé?"

"Yes, Jeffery. But he's in Chicago, he has to be!"

Elijah put a heavy hand on my shoulder. It was rough and callused, but I leaned my cheek against its comfort and warmth.

"I wouldn't be too sure. It's hard on a man, being thrown aside."

I wanted to protest that I hadn't just thrown Jeffery aside, that I'd had good reason to break the engagement, but I was distracted by Philip's station wagon turning into the drive.

"Oh, there's Philip. I do hope he's still speaking to me." I kissed Elijah's rough cheek and ran off to meet my love.

Erna met him first, and I thought she whispered to him, then turned and went back into the kitchen.

I had been prepared to rush into his arms, but something in his eyes held me back. What had Erna said to him, I wondered.

"Lea?" He asked it in the manner of a stranger meeting a stranger.

I stopped, my hands on the gatepost. "I can see," I said slowly, "that I did something terrible last night. Whatever it was, and I have no idea, I hope you'll forgive me. You can't imagine how dreadful it is not to be able to remember what I did to embarrass you. Please say you don't hate me?"

"No, Lea, I don't hate you, and you didn't do anything to *embarrass* me." He leaned rather heavily on the word "embarrass," but I wasn't sure I wanted to know what other word he might have used. "How's the head?"

"All right. I know I deserve a hangover, but I feel fine."

He reached for my hand, and while I would have gone into his arms, he didn't encourage me. "Come on. Let's go for a walk. A little fresh air and exercise should be good for us."

I looked discerningly at him. His eyes were puffy, as if he, too, had overindulged. In fact he looked a good deal the worse for last night, while I looked particularly well. Poor Philip. I squeezed his hand and I got a halfhearted squeeze back. I wouldn't be hurt about it; it was at least partly my own fault.

Erna was watching us from the kitchen door. I called, "Can we pick up anything if we walk to the village?"

"Milk," she said, and went inside.

We used the worn rock steps in the cliff to reach the beach and walked hand in hand and barefoot in the waves. Philip was quieter than usual, but I allowed for that in view of our peculiar evening the night before. I smiled at him and squeezed his hand to let him know I understood. Just as we approached the village his beeper sounded.

"Drat!" he said, savagely shutting it off.

"Go ahead, darling. I'll meet you at the general store when you're finished. I'll just wait as long as I have to. You're getting to be a real doctor. That's two patients in as many days. Soon you'll be rich."

He gave me an inquiring look before he sprinted off across the hard-packed sand.

I dawdled in the sun, walking slowly, swinging my sandals until I came to Erna's house. I was curious to see the inside, probably simply because she was reluctant to have anyone enter. What was in there she wouldn't let anyone see? Maybe she was a terrible housekeeper in her own place, and couldn't afford to have the village find out about her slovenly personal habits, since she made her living by cleaning homes. Or could it be she had a cache of Joanna's things; could that be where her hat and, God forbid, even the hatchet had come from? I was afraid to know, but as I stared at the heavily curtained blank windows in the little white frame house I became even more afraid of not knowing.

I hesitated, my hand on the picket gate. The house would be locked. There was no way I could get inside.

A vision of Mark with his handful of rusted keys flashed into my mind. Would any of the keys to Seven Gates fit her lock? No, even if one would fit I couldn't stand there in broad daylight trying one after another. I moved on slowly. I could always say she had sent me for another lamp should anyone.... But there was no one around, and the windows of the neighboring houses were shut against the sun and summer heat.

I turned back, opened the gate and strode, heart

thumping, up to the front door. Three keys later, wet with perspiration of fear, I stood in the dimness of Erna's tiny living room.

The furniture was old, castoffs, but the house was as neat as it could be, smelling of beeswax and turpentine. I tiptoed furtively into another room, a small Spartan bedroom with a single iron bed, painted white, and a mismatched walnut dresser and desk. Then I saw it!

Hanging over the desk, a dim light shining upon it even in daytime. A portrait. My Cassandra, but younger and with the light of passion mixed with fanatic fervor. I looked for the signature of the artist, but I knew before I saw it. Jay Savage! Did he paint only women who were passionately in love with him, or was no woman safe from his charms or whatever it was that brought out these intense expressions of love?

Erna in love with Joanna's lover! Or Joanna in love with Erna's. Whom had he chosen? Joanna, of course, and I was her image.

I felt stifled, afraid. I careered into unseen furniture as I fought my way out of the dark little house into the hot sunshine. My hand shook, refusing to fit the key into the boxlike lock. I imposed calm upon myself and got the door locked behind me, then after a quick look around I ran down the walk and out the gate. I didn't want to go to the store; I wanted Philip. I wanted to pour out everything: my fears of Joanna's influence on me, my terror that Erna had killed Joanna out of jealousy, that she was going to kill me because I was the reincarnation of her hated rival. I ran, dropping my sandals, stumbling over the rocky path that led to Philip's home and office.

"Philip!" I cried, rushing into the waiting room.

I stopped dead, my heart drawing up into a freezing ball of lead within me.

Philip stared at me over Judy's blond bright head, obviously having just kissed her.

"Lea! Wait!"

But I was through waiting. I ran from the house, from the town, as far as my shaking legs and breath would take me until I collapsed, hidden from everything and everyone by thick tangled bushes. My breath tore raggedly from me as I strained and panted for breath through arid aching sobs.

I screamed, "How can I live!" A sea gull screamed in mockery, over and over, then wheeled and flew away in silence.

"There is no one, no one," I whispered as the quiet closed in with the thick night fog. I had run a long way; it was getting dark and cold. I wanted to be warm, but I didn't move; I couldn't.

I drifted and pulled the dead breath of fog around me like a shroud and shut off my mind.

CHAPTER FOURTEEN

I SAT up in bed with a start.

"Where...for heaven's sake! What am I doing in grandma's lookout room?" My eyes moved down. "And in someone else's nightgown!"

I felt most peculiar, ill, or worse, as if I had overindulged in drink. I slipped out of grandma's bed, automatically turned the telescope toward the ocean as I passed it and went along to my own room. I discovered it was locked and I had to hunt for the key. I found it with all the others on the pine chest in the room where I had been sleeping. I wondered if I might have had a knock on the head, for while I could find no lump, I was headachey and my memory was very hazy.

I found my lingerie in the drawers where I had put it, but my clothes were all missing from the closet. Anger began to clear my head.

"Erna!" I shouted. "Where have my clothes got to? You can't have taken them all to the cleaners at once. Erna!"

A head poked around the door and for a moment I drew back, startled. "Who...oh, it's you! Erna, you look ghastly! Have we all been sick? You look a hundred and four." I peered in the mirror on the vanity. "I don't look ill. But my hair! Somebody's cut my beautiful hair off! Erna, what happened to my hair?

It's so short. I. . . how could it have been cut? What's going on here? Oh, my beautiful hair!" I ran my fingers through the black strands that had been so long I could sit on them. Through tears of rage I glared at Erna, who just stood there with her mouth agape.

"Well, don't stand there gawking! Get my clothes!" Weeping, I collapsed on the bed. The cool satin of the chartreuse bedspread soothed me. I had just done over my room in the latest decor and I loved it. At least that was unchanged.

Erna had disappeared, presumably to get my clothing back where it belonged. I brushed away my tears with the backs of my fingers, crossed to the mirror and stared at my image, most of all my hair. Who had dared to cut it? It must have been because of illness; that's why everything was so strange.

An old man knocked on my open door, averting his eyes as I grabbed the coverlet to hide my body clad only in a thin honey-colored nightgown.

"Who are you?"

"Elijah," he said, surprise opening his eyes so that I saw they were each of a different color.

How odd, I thought. *I know another man who has eyes of the identical colors, but he is much younger and taller and a good deal better-looking.* "Elijah?"

He nodded.

The man I knew was named Eli. This must be an older relative. "What did you want, Elijah?"

"Nothing. I came to see if you needed anything." He stared, almost unblinking.

I pulled my blanket up higher. I said, "All I need are my clothes, and Erna's gone to get them—though why she took them away in the first place, I don't understand. And I must say I don't like it! Now if you don't mind, sir. . . ." I had conveyed my meaning and he left, ducking his head solemnly.

At that moment Erna appeared with blue jeans and a print shirt. I rather liked the soft shirt, as it had a color in it that would have been good with my eyes, but it wasn't mine, and I certainly wasn't going to get dressed up like a man in those denim trousers. I told her so in no uncertain terms. I'm afraid I behaved rather badly, but she stood there staring at me like an idiot and I went into a temper. She withdrew when I shouted, "You know I'm your friend, but when Joanna Brandt has a servant in her house, she expects service! Now get my clothes!"

I plumped onto my bed fuming. "That's what happens when you try to be a friend to an employee; the relationship gets all out of whack." In fact, now that Leanna had gone, I knew I really should sell the old place and move to the city. Then I smiled. I had thought of doing that, but not now, not now that I had found my love.

I leaned back against the pillows and let myself dream. Perhaps now that I knew my true love, my life would be easier. So many men; so hard to decide between them until the right one came along. How dreadful if I had never met him! Who would I have married? Surely not John Wilde, though I had to admit he could set a girl's blood racing dangerously.

The old man Elijah rapped discreetly. "Uh, could I just have your keys a minute. Your clothes are in. . .are in the trunk, and Erna. . . ."

"Trunk? Was I going someplace?"

"Well, maybe so," he said evasively. "The keys. . . ."

I waved a hand at the key ring on the vanity. He picked them up and scuttled off in that queer sideways gait that must run in his family. He had to be a relative of Eli's. Dear old Eli, so tall and strong and faithful.

I decided to wear the jade unicorn pendant Eli had brought me from the Orient. If I could find it. Nothing was where it ought to be.

"Curious," I mused. "We must all have been ill, something going around. And poor Erna does look so dreadful. I am ashamed of myself for screaming at her. I don't know what gets into me sometimes."

She appeared then, laden with clothing. I jumped up and took some of them from her.

"They're terribly wrinkled. Do you feel well enough to iron this?" I held out a jade green cotton suit with a fashionable peplum. I love it because it made my waist look so small. Erna was still standing in the doorway.

"Well, come in. If you don't feel well, go to bed; otherwise help me hang up these things." I really was sorry I had lost my temper; she did look so very old and ill. "Was I sick, Erna? Is that why my hair was cut off?" Her face blurred through the tears in my eyes.

"Very sick, I'd say." Erna spoke for the first time as she edged warily into the room. She hung the clothing quickly, picked up the suit I had spread on the bed. "I'll get this ironed." She hurried out of the room.

"She's acting so peculiarly," I said to myself as I pulled out the vanity bench and sat down. I opened the top drawer of the low blond dresser. At least my makeup hadn't been packed. I used the eyebrow pencil to accentuate the black wings of my sweeping brows and darkened my lips with coral lipstick, which was quite dry. I made a mental notation to replace it, for its flavor interested my lover, though he fussed good naturedly about how difficult it was to remove.

My lips quirked in a dreamy smile as I dusted my nose with face powder. Happiness ran like warm little rivers through my veins. Being truly in love was like nothing else in the world. I would wait as usual this evening on the widow's walk, straining for the sight of Jay's sail.

Erna returned with my suit, her mouth clamped in a straight line. That at least was as it had been lately. There was something bothering her, but I hadn't been able to dig it out of her.

I held out the silver hairbrush and she took it with a hand I thought was trembling. "Really, Erna, I do think you'd better go to bed. I'll just run down and call Dr. Morgan."

"No need. I'm not sick," she barked.

"Well, you mustn't overdo. I feel very well, considering how ill I must have been. My mind's a little hazy, but . . . well, so long as I feel well now."

Erna ran the brush through my hair, and the motion was soothing as always. Perhaps it was better to have my hair a bit shorter after all. It waved about my face and wasn't unattractive, though what my friends would say, I could imagine, especially the men. Yes, attractive as it was with its gentle dark waves catching the light, it wasn't the wealth of beauty it had been, but there was no use crying over spilled milk.

I stepped into the skirt of the suit Erna had pressed

and was adjusting the jacket, admiring the way the jade green released the green in my eyes, when a very good-looking young man appeared at my door. Fancifully I thought of a sun god, for his coloring was sun gold and bronze. He was tall and lean and his face seemed made for smiling, but today it was haunted with shadows. Something was making him unhappy, poor fellow. I made a special effort to smile cheerily.

"Hello, there. Is there something I can do for you?"

Erna stuck her head around the door and I noted with surprise that her untidy bun was grizzled with streaks of gray. She was not going to age well at all. So young to look so old.

She bit off an introduction, threw it at me and left.

I laughed as I held out my hand. "Did she say *Dr.* Philip McCarney? Joanna Brandt. Have you been taking care of me? I feel wonderful, so you must be a very good doctor indeed. But do look after Erna, won't you? I'm sure she's up and around too soon. What laid us so low, for heaven's sake?"

He didn't answer right away. He took my wrist, apparently getting my pulse, and looked narrowly into my eyes, then sighed as he said, "There hasn't been a definite diagnosis as yet. I'm afraid I'm not your doctor; that would be Dr. Smithers."

"Oh, isn't it awful? I don't remember him, either. But I *am* well now!" I knew I shouldn't be looking up at him in the way I was; I'd been told repeatedly that my habit of glancing sideways through my lashes was flirtatious and leading. I quickly looked away. I had some habits to change now that I had made my choice, but Philip McCarney was an unusually attractive man, even if he did have his smiles rationed.

He said cautiously, "Physically you seem well."

"Good!" I settled the peplum over my hips, turned to the mirror and noted with satisfaction how the slimness of my waist was accentuated by this style. "Then I'm off to find my unicorn!"

His bronze eyebrows shot up, indenting a line in his tanned forehead.

"My pendant—a jade unicorn a dear friend gave me."

"Oh."

For a professional man I decided he was awfully distracted and ill at ease. I would like to have offered him comfort in whatever his trouble might be, but I could scarcely ask him about it, so I concentrated on the problem at hand, my pendant.

"Erna! Where's my jade unicorn? I've looked in my box and it's not there."

She came to the doorway and held out her hand. "Here."

"Wherever did you find it?"

"In the pocket of the jeans. I was getting ready to wash them."

I took the pretty ornament. "How extraordinary! Someone wore it without my permission, and look here! It's broken! The chain's been broken!" I cried out in anger and disappointment.

"I never saw it on her!" Erna said sharply, then shook her head and squeezed her eyes together. When she reopened them she stared at me in an unbelieving way. "My God!" she croaked, and ran from the room.

I, too, shook my head, but I wasn't going to discuss my servant with Dr. McCarney. "Whose were those dreadful mannish jeans, I wonder?"

The doctor answered that one with no hesitation. "Lea's."

"Lea? A nurse here?"

I backed away from his eyes, which should have been so sunny, but they raked me with a sudden bleak, probing attention.

"No. Lea is a beautiful girl who has allowed something terrible to happen to her!"

"Oh!" I backed one more step. I was almost afraid of such a display of deep feelings of loss. I tried to put sympathy into my stumbling, inadequate words. "I—I'm so sorry."

"So am I!" he threw at me as he walked out of the room, his lean young shoulders drooping like an old man's.

"Poor man! I'd like to throttle this Lea, whoever she is, for hurting him so. Or maybe she is dead. He was so ambiguous." I felt a peculiar satisfaction in the thought that the Lea who had broken my pendant might be dead. "Yes, I'm sure that's what he meant."

I heard the back screen door slam, and in a few seconds the sound of a car spewing gravel and roaring angrily up the drive.

"Oh, I do hope he doesn't hurt himself any more over that creature, that Lea person. Poor man, poor Philip."

It took most of the day for me to find all my belongings and get my room back in order. Erna had disappeared and left it all on my shoulders. I tried to remember where I had been planning to go, but the last I could recall was being safe in Jay's arms, and his kisses lingered on my smiling, dreaming lips. I longed for nightfall when I would see his sail, golden against the sequined waters of the setting sun.

AT DUSK I RAN up to the widow's walk, elation bubbling like champagne through my body. Jay insisted on this secrecy in our meetings, even though there was no one else at Seven Gates except Erna. I didn't mind running away from the house to be in his arms, for I wasn't ready to share my love and joy, not even with my childhood friend and helper. Not this time.

The sun melted behind the horizon, and the pink and gold darkened to turquoise—to indigo—to navy blue. I paced, holding myself against the chill of the night and the chill of apprehension.

"Why doesn't he come? What has happened to him. Oh, Lord, don't let anything have happened to him!"

I saw a figure move darkly against the moonlit sea. I dashed through the French doors into the lookout room and down the stairs. I was racing toward the cliff when I stopped short.

"Joanna?"

It wasn't Jay. "Yes. Who is it? Oh, Eli?"

"Yes, it's me. You must be freezing. Here." He took off his jacket and hung it around my shoulders. Its long arms flapped in the damp night wind.

"Oh, Eli! Did you see anyone on the beach?" I asked breathlessly.

"Were you looking for somebody special?"

If only he knew how special, I thought, *but I can't let him know.* I stammered a little as I dissembled. "Well, I. . . well, Erna is still out and. . . ."

He stopped and turned from the wind to light a cigarette. I waited for him, shivering.

"I wouldn't expect Erna back, uh, Joanna," he said as he drew on the cigarette so that the red glow lighted his features dimly.

I grabbed his arm. "So she *is* ill! I knew it! She looked so awful."

He hacked out a laugh. "I guess there's no disputing that now."

"Where is she? Where did she go?"

"She's in her—her mother's house," he said slowly, as if he were remembering something from a long time ago. "I came to help you light the lamps."

"Lamps?"

"Uh, the lines are down. You don't have any lights."

"Oh, I don't like that! I have always been afraid of those kerosene lamps. I knocked one over once and...oh, Eli, why does everything have to go wrong!"

He patted my shoulder and we resumed our way toward the dark house. I was afraid to stay alone without power, but most of all I was afraid for Jay. But if he had seen Eli, naturally he would stay away. I was silly to worry. Nothing had happened to him; once before he left without seeing me when Erna had stuck to me like a burr.

Eli held the front door and it was good to get inside out of the chilly wind. "I think I would rather use a couple of candles, Eli. I do hate those lamps!"

"Whatever you say. Are you afraid to stay alone?" His hand felt rough when he reached for mine in the dark hall.

"No," I lied, for I knew if I told the truth he

would offer to stay. "What are you doing here? Is your boat business in Silver City doing so well you're hiring a helper now?" I asked, intending to remind him that he was no longer a smelly fisherman but a man with a business to attend to. It would be a disaster if he should fail, especially now.

I could hear his quick breath in the black silence of Seven Gates. It was a long time before he answered. "The boat business is gone, Joanna." His roughened hand tightened around my wrist.

"Oh, no, Eli! You can't let it go! That would be just too awful for you...and for me, too. I can't let you fail! Do you need money? I...."

Again he gave that single hacking note of laughter. "It's a mite too late for that." He released my wrist. "Do I hear a car?"

"Oh, yes. I wonder who...."

Jay had no car, so my interest in the arrival trailed off.

Eli pressed a book of matches in my hand. "Here, if you don't want the lamp lit, I'll be going. You know where the candles are."

I nodded in the dark and watched the red glow of Eli's cigarette recede down the hall. He stood, an immense black figure nearly filling the doorway, barely outlined by dim starlight.

"I'll leave it open so you can see a little better. Take care." He was gone.

I felt my way toward the kitchen. The lights of the car played hide-and-seek over the wall cabinets, then halted and went out just as I put a match to the fat candle we kept on the table. I went to the back door and held open the screen. "Who is it?"

"John Wilde. Am I to take heart that you meet me

with candlelight?" He used his voice as a caress.

Laughing, I answered, "You never give up, do you, John? No, I'm afraid I'd be greeting anyone by candlelight tonight. That's all I've got."

He kissed my cheek lightly as I stood back to let him enter. "I'd insist you use the front, but I shouldn't want to be responsible if you tripped in the dark and ruined your elegant suit."

"Nor would I wish to be responsible for your lovely neck if you made me ruin my dignity or my clothes. But how are you, my dear, or should I say *who* are you tonight?"

I was used to John's banter. "I'm well, thank you, and still Joanna. Shall we go into the living room? We might gather up the candles on the way. Will you take the candelabra from the sideboard? I'm rather glad you came tonight. There is something I should discuss with you."

I had promised Jay I wouldn't let anyone know about our relationship. He insisted that he must be allowed to finish some mysterious portrait before we made an announcement, a portrait that he had been working on simultaneously with mine. My own now hung in my room, still fresh with the turpentine smell, and I melted inside as I thought of how he had caught my expression of adoration. Jay was a great artist—and a great lover. He was real, sincere, where John was merely practiced.

"Lea. . . ."

I turned on him so swiftly that the flame of the candle died in midair. "That dreadful creature! What do you know about her?"

He raised one black eyebrow. "So that's the way we're playing it." His exotic eyes glittered in the candlelight as he eased gracefully into a wingback chair and made a production of lighting a cigarette. "Are you sure you want to hear about her?"

"Would I have asked if I didn't?" I snapped.

A little frown puckered the carefully tanned forehead beneath that striking silver hair. "Come now, my dear."

I tapped my nails against the wooden arm of the sofa as I settled myself into the curve of it. "Really, John, I wish you wouldn't call me, 'my dear.' It's so affected. Just use my name. Call me Joanna."

"Your asperity crushes me, *Joanna*. I must teach you better manners. As my wife. . . ."

He had come across the room and now sat beside me, pinning me tightly against the sofa arm. I leaned as far away from him as I could.

"Your wife!"

He smiled lazily. "You don't think I mean to let you get away? It's not often a man gets a second chance at the woman he *will* have for his own. You don't think for a moment that young puppy. . . ."

"How dare you call him a young puppy!" I struggled to get up, but I was no match for his leanly muscular body. His mouth searched my face, my eyes, my throat, until it found my mouth and possessed it. I could struggle no longer, and my body slid so that I felt the long heat of his. As his fingers touched the buttons on my thin jacket I tried to cry out Jay's name, but suddenly it slipped away from me, and I could not recall his face.

"John, no!"

"Yes, my little vixen. This time, yes!" His impatient hands tore at the remaining buttons.

A sudden shattering of glass jerked him upward.

''What the hell!'' He was on his feet, closing with a man—I couldn't make out who it was.

I cowered on the sofa as the two struggled in the flickering light. Then I gathered my feet beneath me and bolted, scrambled up the dark stairs and threw myself in my room. I heard the front door slam open and hit the wall, then footsteps pounded hollowly across the porch and thudded into the sand.

''Damn!''

It was John, breathing hard.

I ran to the front window. One of the men was running along the cliff. I stood holding my breath, listening. The house was creaking like a ship in a storm, covering small noises. After what felt like weeks I heard the snarl of John's car as it took off, spitting gravel against the side of the house.

I leaned my cheek against the cool window. John was gone; the intruder was gone. There wasn't one part of me that wasn't shaking. The ring of keys jangled like a musical instrument out of tune as I locked my door. Let the burglar strip the rest of the house if he wanted to. I stayed in my room and spent the night sitting up, fully dressed, on the bed. At first I trembled in terror, but when the intruder showed no inclination toward returning, the humor in it began to bubble up inside me.

''Poor John! He probably thinks he was routed by a jealous lover! Well, I'll never tell him any different. I do hope he did some permanent damage to that expensive suit. It would serve him right!'' I sobered as I thought now I would never be able to be friends again with John. It was too bad. He was so amusing.

When the pale gray dawn made enough light to see

by, I mustered my courage, took my keys, and stole downstairs to lock up.

Who was the man who had rescued me from John? Once more mirth tickled my throat.

"I suppose I should have hit him with something, but then where would I have been?" I glanced down at my cotton jacket, still open, in fact never to be buttoned again, for half of the buttonholes were torn. I was laughing as I prepared, however late, for bed. All in all it had been quite an adventurous night.

I pulled the curtains in my room and crawled sleepily under the chartreuse satin spread. Little bubbles of laughter ran along with me into sleep.

CHAPTER FIFTEEN

A SHARP, insistent rapping wakened me the next day. I got up, trembling a little, and poked my head out the window.

"Who is it?" I called.

"Philip!"

"Philip? Oh, Dr. McCarney! I'll be right down."

I found an ivory satin robe in the closet. I wrinkled my nose as I shrugged into it. It smelled of mothballs.

He crowded into the hall almost before I had the door open, and looked me over quickly and critically. "Are you all right?"

"Of course."

"What happened to the window in the living room?"

"Oh!" My hand flew to my mouth. "I locked the doors, but of course he could have come in through the window—easier the second time."

"Who? What happened?"

The bizarre scene from last night unfolded in my head. My lips quivered, but I held in my amusement the best I could as I told Philip the basics. "I had an intruder who made a most dramatic entrance, through the window, glass flying. Fortunately, Mr. Wilde was here and sent him packing."

"But who was it? Did you get a good look at him?"

"No, I didn't, but, it's all over anyway, except for having the window repaired. I'd better see to that today."

"I'll take care of it," he said absently, his brows drawn together. Finally he shook his head. "You seem to attract trouble. It's uncanny."

"Now, just a minute! I have one peculiar incident and you have the temerity to make a statement like that. I must remind you that we have met exactly once, and for a very short time, so kindly keep your unfounded observations to yourself."

It didn't require much to take the wind out of his sails, I noticed. There was a sudden drop to his shoulders, a pinching in of his nostrils in disappointment or dejection.

"Still Joanna," he observed.

"Always Joanna."

His arms shot out and he shook me violently. "No! I won't let you! Lea! Come out of this game you're playing. For God's sake, stop it before it's too late!"

My satin robe fell open and slipped off my shoulders. "Doctor!"

"Oh, Lea! How can you?" He clutched me hard against his body as violently as he had shaken me. My lips were parted in astonishment when his mouth came down over mine, fierce and hot. I fell back, but he drove me against the wall, his passion rising unleashed as I felt the satin robe slide off my unresisting hands. He had one hand entangled in my hair, holding me prisoner, the other pressed savagely against the small of my back, forcing my body to his. Suddenly he released me, and I sagged against the wall, my eyes closed.

I didn't hear him go; when I opened my eyes he was gone. I saw the puddle of ivory satin at my feet and for a moment it meant nothing to me. The thin straps of my filmy gown had fallen from my shoulders until I was bare to the waist. Slowing I pulled them up, my crossed arms sliding over my hot skin.

"Philip. . . ." My lips felt hot and swollen.

Suddenly a flash of a girl, bright blond hair, pierced my thoughts and I stood up straight, jerking my gown to rights. I picked up the robe from the floor and thrust my arms through the sleeves.

I curled my lips into a mocking smile. "Well, Joanna, you do lead an exciting life lately. What was it he said? You attract trouble? I'm beginning to believe him."

There was a tentative rattle at the back door. I tied the tasseled sash tightly around my waist as I strode into the kitchen. "Who's there?"

"It's me—Erna."

I let her in.

"Muffins," she said, her eyes on the box she held. She filled the coffeepot, set it on the stove and took two eggs out of the red ice chest on the counter.

I noticed the refrigerator door was open, showing empty shelves. We must have been without power for several days.

"I don't think you should be here," I told her. "You should get as much rest as you can."

She put down the saucepan she had filled with water and turned slowly. Her small dark eyes started at my bare feet and traveled discerningly up my body to my face, then fastened onto my own eyes. Her words came out flatly, carefully spaced out in the still, cool air between us.

"I will *never* rest until Joanna Brandt is where she belongs!"

She turned back to the counter, poured a measure of salt into the palm of her hand and dusted it off into the pan of water, then set it on the stove.

I blinked and ran the sentence back through my consciousness. Then I shrugged. Erna was getting stranger and stranger lately.

"I'm going to get dressed."

"You do that," she said in that same flat tone.

I started into the hall, then turned back. "You didn't ask about the window."

"Didn't have to. Doc told me."

I leaned against the doorsill, tapping my chin with my fingers. If I told her the whole story I could shock her out of that cold queerness she was turning on me this morning. "Erna. . . ."

Her flaming eyes burned over my face. "Get dressed! I won't hear any more of your lying games! You got what you deserved once, and don't think you'll escape this time! You killed Jay just as—"

"Killed— Erna what are you talking about! I never hurt anybody. Jay's alive."

"Jay's dead!" Her back was against the stove, her wide-hipped body arching forward, her hands against the white enamel, ready to push her toward me. Her teeth were bared and snarling noises issued from her throat.

I stared, afraid of my old friend. "Erna. . . ."

She didn't move, but stood taut as if ready to spring, her hands curling into yellow talons.

I fled upstairs. "She's gone crazy! I've got to get her out of my house! The whole world's going crazy. My friends are turning on me—John, Erna, even strangers bursting into my house in the most outlandish manner! Why, I'm almost afraid to eat what Erna's cooking! Why does she suddenly hate me so? And saying I killed Jay when he's.... If he'd been killed, I would have heard. She's crazy. I must get the doctor. She must be still terribly ill!"

I grabbed slacks and a blouse out of the closet, paying no attention to my choice, and pulled them on. I ran out the front door and down the cliff face, slipping near the bottom, barely saving myself from a fall to the rocks below. I was out of breath when I arrived at Dr. Morgan's house. I gaped at the new paint. The house looked like a candy box. The shingle hung still; the breeze hadn't begun.

P. McCarney, M.D.

Had Dr. Morgan moved? I burst into the waiting room. It looked reassuringly familiar with its somber furnishings. The girl at the desk looked up, her cool blue gaze taking in my disheveled appearance and breathlessness, and dismissing it.

"Yes?" Her voice was as cool as her eyes.

"The doctor...."

"Isn't in," she finished. "May—"

Angrily, I cut in, "No!" I turned and ran out, my hip painfully clipping the door frame. "Stupid little squirrel!"

I was already out of breath and I slowed, then slumped to the sand. I wasn't keen on going home as long as Erna was in such a mood, but my stomach was sending messages of hunger. I had run off without bringing any money, but I had an account at the little store. I could buy myself a bit of cheese and fruit, and maybe get a line on Dr. Morgan's whereabouts. I ran my fingers through my hair, trying to get the tangles out of it. No, I couldn't go to the store without having my hair brushed at least. Maybe Erna would have left by now; surely if she was that angry, she wouldn't stay.

I took the long way home by the road, giving Erna plenty of time to clear out. The road was narrow. I had never liked walking it, and as people do when they tighten in expectation of a noise, I jumped nearly out of my skin when a horn blared around a curve. A station wagon of some new make screeched to a halt.

"Le...." Philip stopped, seeming confused, then he motioned franctically. "Get in!"

"You can't stop there! Somebody's going to come around the curve and hit you!" I shouted.

"And you're going to get yourself killed standing in the middle of the road! Now get in, damn it!"

He leaned and opened the door on the passenger side. I hesitated, then thought that if I didn't do as he asked he was going to stay there until he became a traffic statistic.

I jumped into the front seat and shut the door, and he took off with a speed that jerked my head back. I compressed my lips in exasperation. "I was going the other way, you know. Home, for something to eat and a comb."

He reached into a back pocket of his snug blue jeans and handed me a small black comb. "I'll take you to lunch," he said tersely.

"No, thank you."

He didn't take his eyes off the road. "Look, I'm sorry about the caveman tactics this morning."

I tried not to remember that fierce embrace, and now that he made me remember, I felt the heat of his body all over even though he wasn't touching me.

I made myself shrug and said flippantly, "Never mind. I think I'm getting used to things like that."

That time he sent a sharp glance my way, but he said nothing.

I was getting the night tangles out of my hair, but I was increasingly aware that I had the vestiges of last night's makeup on my face, as I had never prepared properly for bed.

"I need to wash my face. I can't go into a restaurant this way. Erna's gone berserk, and I left the house in a disreputable state. She actually frightened me. In fact, I was looking for Dr. Morgan. He apparently moved away."

"He did. Erna's all right. I've just seen her. She's moving back to her own house. You'll need to get someone to stay with you."

"I don't need anyone. I. . . ." I had nearly told him about Jay. It would be a blessing to have the house to myself. I could see how I would entertain my love—candles, and food I would cook myself. I tried to imagine his face opposite me at the dining-room table, but it kept slipping just out of focus in my mind.

"Elijah is fixing your window. You haven't forgotten about that, have you? You can't stay there alone."

I patted his knee. "Don't worry so about me, doctor. I promise you I won't be alone."

He had driven through the village and now pulled into the parking lot of a coffee shop. "You can wash your face in the lounge if you want. You look fine to me."

I pulled the rearview mirror over. There was a hint of lipstick outlining my mouth, but considering my night and this ghastly morning, I didn't look too dreadful.

"All right. I'm so hungry that I'm afraid that takes precedence over my lack of makeup." I waited as he came around the car to open my door.

The sun was near its zenith and was beating down hotly. I fanned myself with my hand. "It's really summer."

"Middle of July. It's time," Philip answered calmly.

"Middle of July." Suddenly the sun lost its power for me, and I shook with a teeth-chattering chill.

He put an arm around me. "What is it?"

"I don't know. A chill." I tossed off the feeling. "A goose walking over my grave, I guess."

The middle of July, the middle of July, a freak storm. The words tumbled through my brain as I splashed cold water from the single spigot in the ladies' lounge. I shivered again as I pressed a paper towel to my white cheeks. My eyes looked back at me from the splattered mirror, yellow cat's eyes. They were the eyes of a stranger. I frowned and scolded myself. "You've had too little sleep, too much excitement. Don't try to think."

Philip had ordered for both of us, and a hot steaming cup of coffee waited for me in the red plastic booth in the corner of the glass-walled restaurant. We didn't talk much while we ate; we each made comments about the view of the ocean, and I observed that the place must be fairly new as I had not seen it before. When the waitress had cleared away the dishes we lingered over second cups of coffee.

Philip asked, "Feeling better?"

"Much. Thank you, doctor. Being awake most of

the night and having no breakfast was about to do me in."

"I should be getting back. I have something in mind that I'd like to show you on the way. Are you ready?"

It was pleasant in the restaurant with the sun sending a stream of yellow light across the table between us. I watched dust motes performing a leaping ballet in the spotlight of early afternoon.

He said gently, "I have to go now."

I got up lethargically and he waited and walked with his hand on my shoulder as we left the café.

As we drove back the way we had come, I caught myself staring at Philip's sensitive, though set, lips, and feeling that rush of warmth I had tried to deny. It was too confusing. I was in love with Jay Savage; I scarcely knew Philip. I set my mind to concentrating on the roadside scenery, which was always newly beautiful to me.

The road wound through tunnels of deep green trees, then rose to present an oceanic pageant: glittering water, wheeling white gulls, triangular sailboats scudding along before the fresh breeze. We dipped again into the froth of trees and out where a cliff cut off the panorama with dead trees that looked like tortured witches. I hadn't noticed where we were heading until I saw the open iron gates.

"Philip! The cemetery?"

"Take it easy. There's something here I think you should see." He drove over the uneven stone drive with one hand and held my hand tightly with the other.

"Really! I—"

"Hush. There's nothing here that can hurt you."

"Of course not, but it's hardly my idea of an outing!"

I did feel apprehensive. What on earth did he have in mind?

He stopped the car close to a spirelike monument and came around to help me out. "Come on, hop out."

Reluctantly I took his hand. He nearly pulled me along over the fresh grass.

"No. Philip, I don't want to be here. I don't like it."

He took my shoulders and gripped me hard. "I want you to end this game, Lea. End it now!" He turned me to face the stone, the grave. "Read it, Lea, read the name and date!"

"No!"

"Please, Lea! Open your eyes! Read it!"

He shook me, and I started to scream. "I can't! I can't!" I heard my own screams and the sound shocked me into silence. "Joanna Brandt doesn't scream," I said.

He removed his hands from my shoulders so suddenly that I reeled and came up against the white monument, my fingers clawing the smooth stone, my hair falling wildly into my face.

"You are not Joanna Brandt!"

"I am! I am Joanna!"

And a confirmation came as someone shouted, "Joanna!"

Rough hands helped me to my feet and brushed the hair out of my eyes. It was the old man, Elijah. He shook his huge fist at Philip. "You hurt her and it's the last thing you'll ever do," he roared.

"Elijah—"

"Don't you Elijah me, you young. . . ." He advanced on Philip, breathing danger.

I cried, "Elijah! It's all right! He didn't hurt me. Please, Elijah, just take me home. Please!"

He turned back to me; I quickly took his hand and pulled at it. "Come. Take me home." I pleaded with my eyes, and he gave in to me with a final glare at the frustrated young doctor.

"Elijah, you don't understand what you're doing!" Philip cried. "You must make her see. . . ."

Elijah took my elbow firmly and propelled me forward. "Ain't nothing here she wants to see."

The old man walked so fast I was nearly running at his side. I looked back at Philip, whose face was a study in anger and defeat.

"Lea! Elijah!" Suddenly his expression changed, wiping out the anger with—was it speculation? At that moment I tripped over a stone and had to turn to look where I was going.

"Have you back at Seven Gates where you belong in a jiffy. Don't know what this world is coming to. Why was he throwing you around like that? Never thought Doc would turn mean. What was going on?"

Before I answered I reflected back on the past twenty-four hours. John; the intruder bursting through the glass; Philip's fierce behavior this morning. I stood a little straighter and tugged on Elijah's roughened hand.

"Slow down. He's harmless. I think, Elijah, that the good doctor has developed a passion for me. My goodness, what an exciting time these past few hours have been!" I wouldn't tell Elijah precisely what I meant, although he did press me for details. I sent a flirtatious sidelong glance at him, teasing until he grinned.

"Okay, have your little secrets, but next time you have one of those exciting evenings, fix your own window."

"Oh, you fixed it for me! What an old darling you are!"

"Oh, not so old as to be immune to your charms. But now that you're mad at the doc, that's one less competitor I have to worry about." He threw an arm around me in a companionable way and began to sing an old sea ballad.

I joined him, stumbling over the words until we were laughing so we couldn't sing. He left me on the front porch.

I felt gay and exhilarated as I went upstairs, shedding my clothes on the way. As I soaked in a steamy hot bath, I tried to think of what to wear tonight, for surely Jay would come, but my mind went blank just as I mentally opened my closet. Well, what did it matter? Still, it was odd, those little blank spells; it was as if my soul escaped, leaving me nothing more than an empty body.

I wrapped myself in a towel and went singing to my room. As I opened the door I had an inspiration. I would wear the dress I had worn for my beautiful portrait. Jay would like that.

CHAPTER SIXTEEN

MY PORTRAIT was gone. Even after I had frantically searched the rest of the house, I kept going back to the fireplace in my room, staring disbelievingly at the bare wall over the mantel where it had hung.

"It has to be here! Who would have taken it? It makes no sense!"

Could Jay have decided something wasn't right, that he wanted to do more work on it? Surely he would have at least left a note, yet it was the only explanation I could think of, and that not a very satisfactory one.

I didn't wear the chiffon dress from the portrait as I had planned. When I opened my closet my eye was taken by a rich brown dotted swiss. The ruffles on the neckline partly disguised the deep décolleté plunge, and it clung tightly to my waist, then fluttered away into summery folds. The dress was Jay's favorite. I whirled before the mirror, the late-afternoon sun playing lights and shadows over the rippling skirt. It was a lovely dress.

I sat down on the vanity bench and leaned forward toward the glass to put on my makeup, fussing again over the dry lipstick. Then I leaned closer. Was there something on the dress? The tiny white dots on the neckline ruffle weren't as white as they should be; they were stained a pinkish brown. Or was it a trick of the light?

"Oh, dear. And I did so want to wear this!"

I went back to the closet and fingered through the dresses, pulling out one after another and flinging them back. Nothing pleased me.

"Maybe I can get the stain out." I leaned again toward the mirror, but the light was fading; I could no longer see a stain.

I went to the window and tried to pull the ruffle out so I could see, but even there the light was too dim. There was a closeness to the air, and I opened the window all the way to the top. It was hot, and blue gray clouds swallowed up the last of the sun. The chartreuse draperies hung straight at the window. The breeze had died.

"It can't storm," I muttered to myself. "It just doesn't in the middle of July. Besides, Jay might not put the boat in the water if it is threatening. But that's silly. Of course it won't storm. Not in the summer. It just doesn't."

It was cooler downstairs. I set about making a meager dinner for myself. I thought of Erna's strange anger as I put the cold muffins on the kitchen table. I found a can of soup and heated it. By the time I had sat down to eat, it was already so dark I had to light the candle. As I pushed it back toward the center of the table, my fingers brushed a too smooth place in the deep grain of the oak. I rubbed my hand back and forth over the spot that shone glossier in the candlelight than the rest of the old table.

As my hand passed over it for the second time, a pain shot through my temple. I snatched my fingers away and held my head.

"Oh! Thank goodness, it's going away!"

I wasn't hungry, but I forced myself to eat, for I remembered I had eaten only one meal all day. No doubt that was the cause of the head pain.

I put my few dishes in the sink, then recalled I had no one to wash them except myself. Grimly I set about it, thinking the sooner I went to Silver City and replaced some servants, the better.

I glanced at the clock on top of the silent refrigerator. It was early, but with the prematurely fading light Jay would undoubtedly come early. Sometimes I wished he made more money from his work; he did need a car. There were times, such as tonight, when the sailboat wasn't practical, though he laughed at me when I worried about it. He would say. . . . But just what he said slipped away as I tried to hear his voice. I shrugged lightly. No matter; I would see him and hear his beloved voice very soon.

I was thinking of Erna and her change in attitude toward me as I went up to wait for Jay on the widow's walk. In fact I was so deep in thought that when her face loomed into the light from the candles I screamed.

"Erna!"

Her fanatic's face floated, apparently bodiless, in the dark of the lookout room.

"For heaven's sake, say something!"

I strained to see her better. Her face was raised to a saffron sun shaft that knifed across her shadowed features. She looked as if she were about to make a pronouncement of doom. I took the light closer. "A painting!"

My breathing settled down as I looked closely at the canvas still on the easel. "And a good painting, too!" I searched for the artist's signature. There was none. "Jay? It's certainly good enough, but I don't think it's his." I didn't want it to be Jay's painting. I didn't want him painting other women, not even Erna. That was silly. I couldn't be jealous of Erna, but there was something about the fervent, terrible passion in this face. Then I tossed off a laugh. Jay and Erna? It was ludicrous.

I squeezed out through the French doors, careful not to let the rising wind blow out the little lighting I had in the room behind me. The lightning tore the sky.

Not in the middle of July!

I scanned the dark waters for the white triangle of a sail, but when the flash came again I could see that the ocean was empty except for rollers building up far out to sea and smashing at the foot of the cliff. A hot sullen breath of wind puffed at my face, then fell still.

It would be madness for Jay to put out in weather like this, yet I couldn't force myself to abandon my vigil, for he was daring, perhaps even foolhardy at times. So I paced. The fitful wind turned surly and suddenly all around me lightning flickered snakelike tongues and thunder crashed vehemently. The moist heat turned chill, but still I paced, straining to see. At last a torrent of rain drove me inside, its first few streams driving like sharp fingernails into my skin. The wind robbed the candles of their flames, but I didn't relight them. I pressed my face to the French doors and watched the freak unseasonal storm. It shook its invisible fists at the windows and I saw one of the witch trees torn from the cliff before I ran from the glass.

Searing fire bolts lighted my way into my room

and I flung myself onto my bed. The storm was frightening enough, but my overwhelming fear was for Jay. The tempest raging outside had come up fast, unexpectedly; he might have already been on the water when it hit.

I hugged my sick fear and rocked back and forth. I knew he was dead. There was a queer emptiness in the pit of my stomach, a hollow lump of knowledge. Yet I didn't cry.

Wearily I got up and reached for the side zipper in my dress. The air was damp, and the storm was cooling the house. I numbly moved to the window I had opened earlier. The draperies were sodden, ruined. The wind tore in and my hair flapped in wet tangles as I struggled with the window. When at last it was down, I turned again to my preparations for bed.

Over the rappings of the fury I heard a different sound, a nearer sound. It scraped closer and closer. I held my breath and listened. Was it someone coming slowly up the stairs? No, the scraping, scraping, came from a different direction.

"It's just the wind in the chimney."

Yet it neared, shuffled. The room was dark; the thunder a far-off rumbling.

Had the intruder returned? Surely the sound was someone on the stairs, and it was a trick of the wind that made it seem to come from behind the fireplace.

"Who's there?" My words were small chirpings in the sounds of the furious night.

Silence.

My fingernails drove into my palms as I waited.

Nothing.

It was imagination or the wind. I walked stiffly to the bed and pulled the spread back. A good night's sleep would put my nervous fancies back into perspective.

My back was to the fireplace. A double flash of receding lightning threw a shadow on the wall. I was too terrified to scream. There was a figure, someone who was coming slowly toward me. I whirled, holding my arms before my face, my eyes futilely wide in the inky darkness. I tried to make some sound, any sound, but cold snakes of terror twisted and rose inside me, closing my throat.

"Joanna?" The voice was a rough whisper.

Still I was frozen, unable to breath, unable to move.

"Please, Joanna. Where are you?"

Suddenly I realized that he hadn't seen me in the flash as I had seen his shadow. There was a chance. If I could get to the door.... But when he whispered again, I knew he had cut off that escape. I turned to face the whisperer.

I backed away, feeling behind me for a lamp, anything for a weapon. If I could get to the fireplace, the poker....

Lightning lit the room, the black figure lunged and rough hands clutched at me, arms closed around me, pinning me into a suffocating embrace. My face was forced against the man, against a rough shoulder. I tried to suck in air, but I couldn't get my breath. My arms were useless, pinned to my sides. At last I got my head twisted enough to the side to gasp a breath. An odor sent my senses reeling.

"Mothballs!"

I hadn't realized I had spoken aloud until the arms dropped away from me.

"Sorry if I've offended you—again." The voice was cracked, unrecognizable.

Hope sent messages of strength to my quivering legs. Keep him talking, edge away toward the door.

The sandpaper hand grasped my arm. "No."

I tried to moisten my lips with a dry tongue. "Please. Who are you?"

"Don't try any of your games with me, Joanna. You know damned well who I am!"

"I—I don't. I can't see. Let me turn on the light."

"Light a candle, then. But don't make for the door. I don't want to hurt you." His choked voice ended the final sentence with something like a sob.

I calmed down a little. I tried to make my mind work. Where were the candles? On the mantel. Matches. My quaking fingers dropped the first burning match.

"Here, let me do it for you."

The candle took flame, lighting up the old man's craggy face. "Now you see who it is."

I went limp with relief and sagged onto the bed. "Oh, Elijah! You have no idea how you frightened me."

"I never meant to." He set the flame on the table by the bed and sat down beside me.

Again the smell of strong moth killer assailed my nostrils, and I wrinkled my nose.

"I should have aired it. I'm sorry. I didn't realize...." He left the sentence unfinished, giving his attention instead to my face.

I, in turn, looked at him. A dark suit hung awkwardly on his body. It had been packed away for a long time, and in the meanwhile his powerful body had wasted with age, though he was still a big man. His gnarled hands crept up to the knot of the dark tie. He pulled on it in the way men do when they are unused to a buttoned collar.

Nervously I picked at the dots on my dress. I wanted to ask him what he was doing in my room, but I was afraid. Ridiculous to be afraid of old Elijah. Instead I said, "You're very dressed up."

"I bought this suit for our wedding." His eyes glittered yellow in the light from the one candle.

"Our wed—"

"Joanna!" His hands grasped my shoulders and turned me to him as he buried his face in the ruffles on my breast.

I jerked away. "Elijah! Don't!"

His grasp tightened and I felt his cracked old lips on my throat. I choked as I inhaled the odor from the awful old suit. "No!"

"Please, Joanna. . . ."

A picture of a bronze head bending over a bright blond one, and a searing hurt tore at me. I slammed my mind shut.

"Elijah!"

"Please, Joanna. You told me you'd marry me when I was in a decent business, didn't stink of fish. I docked my boat. I sat all day in a fancy showroom waiting for your rich friends to come in and. . . ." He was sitting up, hands like crab claws biting into my shoulders. My head flopped as he shook me. Then he gathered me to his chest and silently rocked me, a groan escaping his tortured mouth.

Sickness filled my whole body. Elijah and Joanna. I would never have believed that pity and horror could live in my emotions at the same time, but I was weeping for Elijah's terrible crippling hurt as I wept with terror for my life.

"Oh, Joanna, Joanna. You can't leave me!"

I struggled to free my head. "Elijah! Please! I am not Joanna."

Again the picture of Philip kissing Judy appeared on my mind. "I am not Joanna."

He paid no attention. "You are coming away with me, Joanna. There is nothing for you here. There's nothing left."

I glanced toward the door. I would have to get him off guard, then run for it and pray it wasn't locked. "I don't understand, Elijah," I said to keep him talking.

"I mean your artist. He's gone."

"Gone? Gone where?" My eyes were still on the area between me and the way out.

His voice cracked as he said, "I mean he's dead. The boat will wash up and they'll blame the storm. . . ."

The sledgehammer of truth hit my stomach at the same moment the lightning flared and struck a gleam from what leaned against the door.

I leaped, breaking his hold, but he threw himself between me and my avenue of escape and the instrument of my death. I moved my wrists, but I couldn't break his grip.

"I don't want to hurt you! Just come with me. Give me a chance. I've given up everything, but I won't give you up. I won't!"

"I am not Joanna!" I screamed. "I'm not!"

"Don't tell me I'm old again. Please!"

"I am not Joanna, you murderer!" I fought with strength and fury and I broke his hold. I bolted for the door, but he was in front of me. The lightning flickered on the ax head. I threw myself to the side, falling to the floor. The ax bit into the footboard of the bed, then gleamed as it was jerked upward.

Someone yelled, "Drop it!"

A figure appeared beside the fireplace.

Elijah growled, and I could see spittle shining on his chin as he turned to face the new menace.

"Elijah! No!" I screamed.

I didn't see the gun, only a flash of fire. The sound was lost in a crash of thunder. The ax fell, and the old man spun around.

"There he goes! For God's sake, get out of my way!"

"Philip!"

He leaped over me where I lay on the floor. I heard clattering and shouting.

A small figure bent over me. "You okay?"

"Mark! What are you. . . ?"

"You okay? Did he hurt you?" The boy was screaming it.

I sat up. "I'm all right."

He bolted for the door. I grabbed him by the collar. "Mark! Don't!"

He pulled loose. "Let go, for cryin' out loud. Doc needs help!"

He bolted for the door with me at his flying heels. I followed him outside into the dark, driving rain.

"Where is he? Where's Philip?" I cried, making panicky rushes in all directions at once.

"There! There he is on the cliff!" He pointed in the flash and blur of faraway lightning.

Mark and I shouted at the same time.

"Where did he go, Doc?"

"Philip! Are you all right?"

He answered both of us with a sharp command. "Get back inside! Go!"

There was no arguing with the tone of his voice, but Mark stubbornly stood his ground. I hesitated for a moment, staring into the downpour. Philip was pacing the cliff, looking down into the raging water.

"Come on, Mark," I said, urging him along with a hand on his shoulder. "I think we can help best by making some coffee and getting some heat in the kitchen."

"But, what if that old murderer sneaks up on him from behind? Oh, I wish I had a gun!"

From the shelter of the veranda I looked back once more at Philip. He walked slower, up and down the cliff top, vaguely silhouetted against the dark sky, lighted now and again by the weakening flashes from the storm.

My dress was plastered against me by the freezing-cold rain, and my teeth began to chatter violently. "Come inside, Mark. I don't think Philip needs our help anymore." Hot tears mingled with the icy rain running down my face.

The boy's white face turned up and we looked at each other in the darkness, seeing only vague features, but with unspoken understanding.

"Yeah. Better make that coffee," he said, and led the way to the kitchen.

I remembered the candle burning upstairs in Joanna's room. I shuddered with a sudden violence as the scene just over thrust itself upon my thoughts. I had a lot to answer for, but now wasn't the time to consider that. I spoke bravely through a fear so terrible it threatened to shatter me.

"I've got to get the candle, Mark, before it starts a fire."

He said quickly, "I'll go with you."

"No. There are matches on the table, and a candle. If you can start the coffee. . . I'll be right back." I left quickly, before I could talk myself out of it.

The candle still burned, throwing dim golden light on the shattered bed, the ax lying ineffectual, spent, on the floor. There was a black space, floor to ceiling, in the wall beside the fireplace.

I had found my seventh gate, as Joanna had before me, and nearly with the same results. Would I find, also, the veil through which I might not see? Or had I seen through it? Had Joanna stepped through that mystic seventh gate? Or had I used her to escape from a life I didn't want to face? I didn't know, and that was as frightening as facing poor Elijah with his ax.

I walked very slowly down the stairs toward the kitchen. I heard voices and smelled fresh coffee, but I wasn't eager to face the people I had hurt, much as Joanna had before me.

CHAPTER SEVENTEEN

ERNA SAT at the table, her elbows propped, hair hanging lank and wet. Philip and Mark crowded around the gas oven that was warming the room. Only Mark met my eyes.

"I wouldn't let Doc take me home till I saw you were okay," he said, his sea-colored eyes looking at me anxiously.

Philip examined the rim of his coffee cup with a finger. "You have this young man to thank for your life. Tell her about it, Mark. Then you'd better get home and face the music."

"Yeah. Ma's going to be awful mad, but I had to do it. You remember those footprints in the dust over at the first-mate's house?" He carefully poured a cup of coffee and handed it to me.

I nodded, trying to control my trembling so I wouldn't slop the hot liquid as I sipped.

"Well, I looked at them good and they showed a cut on the sole of one shoe. So Ollie and me, we looked to match them up, and sure enough, we saw the same footprint on the beach and followed it right up to Elijah's house. Well, we ran and told the Doc, but he said it didn't mean anything, that Elijah had to put the hatchet somewhere. But we figured since he was a mean old man, he'd be just the kind who'd chop up a table or a person; wouldn't make him no never-mind. He had a funny kind of temper, like that one day we was here. So mad he couldn't see straight, until he saw you, then he smiled all over his face. So we just went back and stole the hatchet. Should have figured that wouldn't stop him."

"Poor old man," I said.

"Poor old man! He like to split your head open! Anyway, we took to following him. Then one day his tracks ended like he'd clumb right up the side of the house."

"Climbed."

He gave me a disgusted look. "You're getting back to normal, all right. But Ma butted in before we could investigate. I like to never found the way in behind all those bushes in the dark. Well, I knew he had that ax, see. Saw him rip it out of that chopping block behind his house, so I had to get Doc. If I'd've had a gun. . . ."

Philip came to stand beside the boy.

"If you'd had a gun, I suppose you'd have gone all the way by yourself?"

Mark looked wide-eyed. "Sure. You gonna take me home now?"

"Yes. I'll see if I can run a little interference between you and your mother—providing, young man, you promise you'll never do a thing like this again. Hear me?"

Mark shrugged. "Sure. Ain't like to be any more murders around her anyway." He stuck his hands in his pockets and headed for the back door.

Philip turned to me, but his eyes were busy with something over my left shoulder. "I'm going to take him home, then I'll change into dry clothes. Do you want me to come back?"

All I could manage was a nod. My throat ached with hurt, for now I couldn't deny the meaning of Philip's kissing Judy. I had to face it and make the best of whatever happened.

I turned to Erna when the back door shut behind him. Her eyes flickered toward me, wary and non-committal.

"I'm sorry, Erna," I said after a long silence between us.

"Which one? Which one's sorry?"

"Me. Lea. I don't know what to say. I don't think it was ever Joanna. I think I just did it because. . . I'm not sure. Elijah killed her, you know. He loved her, and she hurt him terribly."

"So he killed her. We all get hurt."

"But we don't all kill because of it."

I thought of old Elijah in his carefully preserved wedding suit, the decrepit fishing boat he could neither use nor give up, the waiting day after day in the fancy showroom for customers who never came. Hot tears spilled down my face.

"Here, here!" Erna jumped up.

"Oh, Erna, Joanna was so cruel!"

She looked surprised, then she sat down slowly. "She never meant to be. She couldn't help it. It's just that we all spoiled her. She was so special and I guess we got a kick out of her—well, her spirit, I suppose you'd call it."

"Spunk," I said.

She leaned back. At last she spoke. "I'll never forgive myself for that. If I hadn't called you down for not being more like her. . . ."

I shook my head. "No. It wasn't your fault. I had already started the—game—the escape, whatever it was. And you were right. It was spunk I needed. The spunk to face things instead of pretending. . . oh, I don't know. I always took the easiest way, even with mother. It was always easier to play nursemaid to her—to fetch and carry and spoil her—than to tell her I wanted my own life. I suppose I let her use me, though I'm sure she never meant to."

We were busy with our own thoughts for a while, then Erna spoke slowly.

"Yes, they seemed so opposite, yet in that way I believe they were a lot alike. They never meant any harm, but somehow they took people over."

I shuddered at that phrase. I wondered if I would ever know for certain about Joanna, about myself.

Briskly Erna got up. She felt in her wild hair for hairpins and wound up her straggly bun. "Better get you into some dry clothes or Doc will have my head. If you've got a wrapper or something that'll fit me. . . ."

"I'm sure I have. Come along. It will feel good to get into my own clothes, to be myself."

We walked together into the lookout room.

"Your portrait. You never said if you liked it."

We both looked at it a long time. Finally she spoke.

"It's good, you know. I haven't seen talent like that since. . . not for a long time. You're a real artist, not a card painter. You know that."

"I do know it—now. Thank you."

I handed her a gathered red robe. She took it silently and left the room. Her staunch shoulders drooped, and I knew she was thinking of Jay Savage, of Joanna, of her long-ago lost love. It would do no good to tell her the truth of what had happened to him; perhaps she had already guessed.

I WAS STANDING before the opening in the wall in Joanna's room, a lamp thrust into the darkness beyond, when Philip returned.

"So you've found your seventh gate."

I turned slowly. "And Elijah. He has found his seventh gate, too, hasn't he?"

"I'm afraid so. He tried to take the cliff steps. He must have known. . . ."

"I'm sure he did."

"He may never be found. Those storm waters. . . ."

"Yes. Just like Jay Savage. Just like Jay."

Philip had the same wariness in his eyes that Erna had shown.

"It's really all right, Philip. I know who I am."

"Who?" he asked bluntly.

"Lea Bond. And I intend to keep it that way."

He took the lamp from me and held it between us. "Do you think you can, Lea? Do you believe you can control whatever it is that happens to you?"

I wanted to tell him I could do anything if I were certain of his love and understanding, but his eyes in the lamplight were narrow and probing, not like the sunny, laughing eyes of the Philip who had kissed me in the picnic grotto just a few days before. No doubt those kisses now belonged to Judy; I had to accept that and the hurt that went with it. As Erna had said, we all get hurt.

I said to Philip, "I can't know if I can control it; I can only try. Now, I want to see my so-called seventh gate. Then I will close it forever."

He walked ahead of me, lighting the tiny cubicle behind the fireplace.

"Here's Joanna's portrait! Oh, Philip! He started to slash it. See, there's a tear in it." I lifted the picture to bring it out into the light of the room beyond. "And that's how he hung it in the landing! Look!"

"A long wire. I suppose there's a nail in the moulding at the ceiling. What's in the box?"

I lifted out a long satin nightgown. "I would guess it's a box of Joanna's things intended for charity. That's how he set up the—incidents."

Philip dragged out the box. "Do you want to see the stairs, or are you ready to close it up?"

"Let's close it. I'll get . . . I'll have to hire someone to seal it." I gave a long shuddering sigh. "You know, I almost said, I'll get Elijah to fix it. It's so hard to get used to. Poor Elijah."

Philip was running his hands over the simple trim on the fireplace mantel. "Must be something here to close it. Ah, here it is." The wall panel slid soundlessly into place, and I had to look hard to see that it was any different from the rest of the painted paneling.

"Let's go, Philip. Erna has some coffee, and I expect you could use some."

He stopped me in the hall at the head of the stairs. "Do you feel like talking about it?"

I shook my head. "Not yet. But I will say this; Joanna hurt Elijah cruelly."

"And I suspect I hurt you," he said, taking me by the shoulders and turning me to face him.

My first instinct was to deny it, to save my pride, to pretend I had never seen him kissing Judy Garnett. I forced out the hurt-filled words one by one. "It did hurt me when I saw you. . . ."

He finished for me. "Kissing Judy." He drew my head to his shoulder. "Oh, darling, I'm so sorry. *I* knew it was nothing, but I should have realized how it would look to you.'' He put me away from him and tipped up my chin. ''Look at me, Lea.''

I looked with tear-dimmed eyes into his.

''Judy is leaving. She is getting married; someone she's been in love with for a long time. It's you I love, so much I couldn't bear it when you. . . went away.''

I threw myself into his arms. ''Oh, Philip,'' I sobbed, ''I'll never allow myself to do that again. I'll do anything, go to a hospital, whatever I have to do, but I promise I'll be myself, just me.''

Our tears mingled as his lips tenderly took mine. There would be no searching beyond myself for happiness. I had my talent, Philip's love, and above all a new belief in myself. I didn't need more.

Philip tipped up my chin. ''It's not going to be easy. Whatever happened may threaten you anytime things seem too much to face.''

I nodded. ''I'm aware of that, but I think painting, really painting what I feel instead of denying myself, will help. But Joanna has had her last dance, Philip. Let's put her back in her place, there on the wall.''

My love removed the long thin wire from the painting frame and hung the portrait above the mantel. Joanna smiled out at us.

I said, ''It's a very fine painting, Philip. Nothing more.''

I held out my arms to him and he came to me.

ROBERTA
LEIGH
World-favorite bestselling
author of romance brings you...
LOVE MATCH
The poignant and passionate love story of
Suzy Bedford, a pretty, young journalist
whom experience had taught to be wary of men, and
Craig Dickson, an international tennis star as notorious
for his games off the court as for those on....
352 pages of great romance
reading for only $2.95!
Available now wherever
paperback books are sold.
LM-N

1. How do you rate ______________________________ ?
(Please print book TITLE)

1.6 ☐ excellent
.5 ☐ very good
.4 ☐ good
.3 ☐ fair
.2 ☐ not so good
.1 ☐ poor

2. How likely are you to purchase another book in this series?

2.1 ☐ definitely would purchase
.2 ☐ probably would purchase
.3 ☐ probably would not purchase
.4 ☐ definitely would not purchase

3. How do you compare this book with similar books you usually read?

3.1 ☐ far better than others
.2 ☐ better than others
.3 ☐ about the same
.4 ☐ not as good
.5 ☐ definitely not as good

4. Have you any additional comments about this book?

______________________________ (4)

______________________________ (6)

5. How did you *first* become aware of this book?

8. ☐ read other books in series
9. ☐ in-store display
10. ☐ TV, radio or magazine ad
11. ☐ friend's recommendation
12. ☐ ad inside other books
13. ☐ other ______________ (please specify)

6. What *most* prompted you to buy this book?

14. ☐ read other books in series
15. ☐ friend's recommendation
16. ☐ picture on cover
17. ☐ title
18. ☐ author
19. ☐ advertising
20. ☐ story outline on back
21. ☐ read a few pages
22. ☐ other ______________ (please specify)

J1

7. What type(s) of paperback fiction have you purchased in the past 3 months? Approximately how many?

	No. purchased		No. purchased
☐ contemporary romance	(23) ____	☐ espionage	(37) ____
☐ historical romance	(25) ____	☐ western	(39) ____
☐ gothic romance	(27) ____	☐ contemporary novels	(41) ____
☐ romantic suspense	(29) ____	☐ historical novels	(43) ____
☐ mystery	(31) ____	☐ science fiction/fantasy	(45) ____
☐ private eye	(33) ____	☐ occult	(47) ____
☐ action/adventure	(35) ____	☐ other	(49) ____

8. Have you purchased any books from any of these series in the past 3 months? Approximately how many?

	No. purchased		No. purchased
☐ Harlequin Romance	(51) ____	☐ Harlequin American Romance	(55) ____
☐ Harlequin Presents	(53) ____	☐ Superromance	(57) ____

9. On which date was this book purchased? (59) ______________

10. Please indicate your age group and sex.

61.1 ☐ Male
.2 ☐ Female
62.1 ☐ under 15
.2 ☐ 15-24
.3 ☐ 25-34
.4 ☐ 35-49
.5 ☐ 50-64
.6 ☐ 65 or older

Thank you for completing and returning this questionnaire.

PRINTED IN CANADA

NAME____________________
(Please Print)

ADDRESS____________________

CITY____________________

ZIP CODE____________________

NO POSTAGE
STAMP
NECESSARY
IF MAILED
IN THE
UNITED STATES

BUSINESS REPLY MAIL

FIRST CLASS **PERMIT NO. 70** **TEMPE, AZ.**

POSTAGE WILL BE PAID BY ADDRESSEE

NATIONAL READER SURVEYS

1440 SOUTH PRIEST DRIVE
TEMPE, AZ 85266